# ROALD DAHL's

# Mischief
## AND MAYHEM

# Puffin Books by Roald Dahl

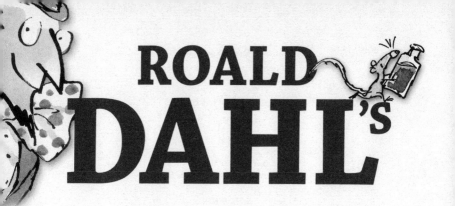

# ROALD DAHL's

# Mischief
## AND MAYHEM

Compiled by **Kay Woodward**

PUFFIN BOOKS
An Imprint of Penguin Group (USA)

**PUFFIN BOOKS**

Published by the Penguin Group

Penguin Group (USA) LLC

375 Hudson Street

New York, New York 10014

USA * Canada * UK * Ireland * Australia

New Zealand * India * South Africa * China

penguin.com

A Penguin Random House Company

Published in Great Britain by Penguin Books Ltd., 2013

First published in the United States by Puffin Books,

an imprint of Penguin Young Readers Group, 2015

Text copyright © 2013 by Roald Dahl Nominee Ltd

Illustrations copyright © 2013 by Quentin Blake

Extracts taken from: *James and the Giant Peach* first published 1961; *Matilda* first published 1988; *Charlie and the Chocolate Factory* first published 1964; *Boy* first published 1984; *The Wonderful Story of Henry Sugar and Six More* first published 1977; *The BFG* first published 1982; *The Enormous Crocodile* first published 1978; *George's Marvellous Medicine* first published 1981; *Danny the Champion of the World* first published 1975; *The Witches* first published 1983; *Fantastic Mr Fox* first published 1970; *Revolting Rhymes* first published 1982; *The Twits* first published 1980; *Charlie and the Great Glass Elevator* first published 1972

Puffin Books ISBN 978-0-14-751355-7

Printed in the United States of America

1 3 5 7 9 10 8 6 4 2

# Introduction

## STOP!

**Yes, you. Stop right there. Don't move.**
Are you an adult? Oh, dear. I'm sorry. This book
is absolutely **NOT** meant for you. Kindly close
the pages and go and do something grown-up
instead. (Perhaps you could make a roast dinner
with a hundred vegetables or creosote a fence or
something.) Off you go. Have they gone? Good.
Hello, non-adult! This book is meant for **YOU**.
But be warned. It contains **mischief** and
**mayhem** of such extreme naughtiness that you
will need the cunning of Fantastic Mr Fox and the
cleverness of Matilda to continue. *You're* cunning
AND clever? Excellent. We'll get along just fine.
**Now, read on.**

If you've bought, borrowed or been given this **TRULY NAUGHTY** book, then you surely already know of Roald Dahl. But, just in case you're one of the 27 people on the planet who haven't heard of him, let me tell you a little more.

# ROALD DAHL *was* **ONE** *of* THE BEST STORYTELLERS EVER.

There. Done. I beg your pardon? You'd like to know even more than that? Well, why didn't you say so?

**Roald Dahl** was born in Wales in 1916 to Norwegian parents. He had four sisters. Sadly, both his father and his eldest sister died when he was very young. And then when he wasn't much older – just nine years old – his mother sent him away to boarding school in England. Roald Dahl hated it so much that he pretended to have appendicitis so that he would be sent home. He *was* sent home.

## Hurray!

But when he was found out he was sent back to school again.

## Boo.

In between detention and homework and being achingly homesick, Roald spent the rest of his school years trying to outwit his **VERY STRICT** teachers and the **FORMIDABLE** matron. And testing new chocolate bars for a **VERY FAMOUS** chocolate company. Luckily, he also loved making up stories. (He wrote it all down in a book called *Boy*, if you'd like to find out EVEN MORE.)

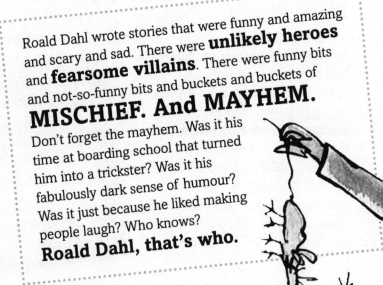

The rest of Roald Dahl's life is like something out of a storybook too. He worked in London, which was chilly, and Africa, which wasn't. He flew fighter-planes in the Second World War, which was very scary. (Unfortunately, he crashed one in the desert, which was even scarier.) He was a spy. Shhhh. And THEN he became a writer. **Phew.**

Roald Dahl wrote stories that were funny and amazing and scary and sad. There were **unlikely heroes** and **fearsome villains**. There were funny bits and not-so-funny bits and buckets and buckets of **MISCHIEF. And MAYHEM.**

Don't forget the mayhem. Was it his time at boarding school that turned him into a trickster? Was it his fabulously dark sense of humour? Was it just because he liked making people laugh? Who knows?

**Roald Dahl, that's who.**

Perhaps you've already read some of Roald Dahl's books? (If not, why not? Go to your nearest library straight away, please.) If so, you'll know that they are chock full of **HILARIOUS tricks**. Have you ever read one of his particularly mischievous tricks and – after checking that no one is watching you, of course – thought, *I could do that*? You have? Marvellous. The thing is MOST GROWN-UPS have read Roald Dahl's books too. (And if they haven't, then they're obviously numpties and not worth tricking.) So the last thing you want to do is copy one of his tricks exactly, because everyone will be expecting you to, say, superglue a hat to their head or turn their hair platinum blond just like Matilda. However, if you take one of Roald Dahl's tricks and turn it into something just a **LITTLE BIT** different, then the results can be

# AMAZING.

Go on, do it.
Roald Dahl would.

**PS** The tricks and pranks and japes and jokes and jests and stunts in this book have been given a star rating to indicate the level of difficulty.

## ☆ TRiCK

One-star tricks are for **total beginners** in the art of trickery.

## ☆☆ TRiCK

Two-star tricks are for more **experienced tricksters** and pranksters.

## ☆☆☆ TRiCK

Three-star tricks should only be attempted by magicians, conjurers, professional jokers, astrophysicists or **senior members of MI6 and the FBI**. Approach with caution (and a member of the armed services, if you have one handy).

*In which James and his friends trick a flock of
seagulls into giving them a lift.*

In a few minutes everything was ready.

It was very quiet now on the top of the peach. There
was nobody in sight – nobody except the Earthworm.

One half of the Earthworm, looking like a great,
thick, juicy, pink sausage, lay innocently in the sun for
all the seagulls to see.

The other half of him was dangling down the
tunnel.

James was crouching close beside the Earthworm
in the tunnel entrance, just below the surface, waiting
for the first seagull. He had a loop of silk string in his
hands.

The Old-Green-Grasshopper and the Ladybird
were further down the tunnel, holding on to the
Earthworm's tail, ready to pull him quickly in out of
danger as soon as James gave the word.

And far below, in the great stone of the peach, the Glow-worm was lighting up the room so that the two spinners, the Silkworm and Miss Spider, could see what they were doing. The Centipede was down there too, exhorting them both frantically to greater efforts, and every now and again James could hear his voice coming up faintly from the depths, shouting, 'Spin, Silkworm, spin, you great fat lazy brute! Faster, faster, or we'll throw you to the sharks!'

'Here comes the first seagull!' whispered James. 'Keep still now, Earthworm. Keep still. The rest of you get ready to pull.'

'Please don't let it spike me,' begged the Earthworm.

'I won't, I won't. Ssshh . . .'

Out of the corner of one eye, James watched the seagull as it came swooping down towards the Earthworm. And then suddenly it was so close that he could see its small black eyes and its curved beak, and the beak was open, ready to grab a nice piece of flesh out of the Earthworm's back.

'Pull!' shouted James.

The Old-Green-Grasshopper and the Ladybird gave the Earthworm's tail an enormous tug, and like magic the Earthworm disappeared into the tunnel. At the same time, up went James's hand and the seagull flew right into the loop of silk that he was holding out. The loop, which had been cleverly made, tightened just the right amount (but

not too much) around its neck, and the seagull was captured.

'Hooray!' shouted the Old-Green-Grasshopper, peering out of the tunnel. 'Well done, James!'

Up flew the seagull with James paying out the silk string as it went. He gave it about fifty yards and then tied the string to the stem of the peach.

'Next one!' he shouted, jumping back into the tunnel. 'Up you get again, Earthworm! Bring up some more silk, Centipede!'

'Oh, I don't like this at all,' wailed the Earthworm. 'It only just missed me! I even felt the wind on my back as it went swishing past!'

'Ssshh!' whispered James. 'Keep still! Here comes another one!'

So they did it again.

And again, and again, and again.

And the seagulls kept coming, and James caught them one after the other and tethered them to the peach stem.

'One hundred seagulls!' he shouted, wiping the sweat from his face.

'Keep going!' they cried. 'Keep going, James!'

'Two hundred seagulls!'

'Three hundred seagulls!'

'Four hundred seagulls!'

The sharks, as though sensing that they were in danger of losing their prey, were hurling themselves at the peach more furiously than ever, and the peach was sinking lower and lower still in the water.

'Five hundred seagulls!' James shouted.

'Silkworm says she's running out of silk!' yelled the Centipede from below. 'She says she can't keep it up much longer. Nor can Miss Spider!'

'Tell them they've *got* to!' James answered. 'They can't stop now!'

'We're lifting!' somebody shouted.

'No, we're not!'

'I felt it!'

'Put on another seagull, quick!'

'Quiet, everybody! Quiet! Here's one coming now!'

This was the five hundred and first seagull, and the moment that James caught it and tethered it to the stem with all the others, the whole enormous peach suddenly started rising up slowly out of the water.

'Look out! Here we go! Hold on, boys!'

But then it stopped.

And there it hung.

It hovered and swayed, but it went no higher.

The bottom of it was just touching the water. It was like a delicately balanced scale that needed only the tiniest push to tip it one way or the other.

'One more will do it!' shouted the Old-Green-Grasshopper, looking out of the tunnel. 'We're almost there!'

And now came the big moment. Quickly, the five hundred and second seagull was caught and harnessed to the peach-stem . . .

And then suddenly . . .

But slowly . . .

Majestically . . .

Like some fabulous golden balloon . . .

With all the seagulls straining at the strings above . . .

The giant peach rose up dripping out of the water and began climbing towards the heavens.

But don't do that, do THIS!

# ☆ TRICK

## The Booby-trapped Peach

Unless you happen to have a giant-fruit-and-veg shop nearby, you're unlikely to have a giant peach. (Or a giant earthworm, for that matter.) **DON'T PANIC**. For this trick, you will need one average, run-of-the-mill, really quite normal-sized peach, available from all good fruit-and-veg shops. But it must be VERY RIPE.

Why did the peach stop at the top of the hill? **Because it ran out of juice.**

### YOU WILL NEED:

☆ One ripe peach
☆ One jelly worm (the edible sort)
☆ One cocktail stick or a toothpick
☆ One fruit bowl

14

## WHAT YOU DO:

**1** Being VERY careful, **spear your peach** with a cocktail stick or toothpick and wiggle it about a bit so that you've made a small tunnel in your sticky, juicy fruit.

**2** **Poke the jelly worm into the tunnel**. Leave a little bit of the worm sticking out of the peach, just like in *James and the Giant Peach*.

**3** Put the **booby-trapped peach** into the fruit bowl.

**4** # Wait.

**5** If a grown-up does not immediately decide that they would like to sink their teeth into a delicious peach then you may have to **fill their heads with fruity, sticky, juicy thoughts** until they can stand it no longer and simply have to eat a peach RIGHT NOW.

**6** Get ready to double up with laughter when the grown-up bites into the ripe peach and thinks they have eaten **A REAL LIVE EARTHWORM**.

**7** **Double up with laughter. Or run.**

From Matilda

# The Platinum-Blond Man

*In which Matilda swaps OIL OF VIOLETS HAIR TONIC for PLATINUM BLONDE HAIR-DYE EXTRA STRONG and makes her father see RED. Actually, yellow. Hmm. Blond, really.*

Mr Wormwood kept his hair looking bright and strong, or so he thought, by rubbing into it every morning large quantities of a lotion called OIL OF VIOLETS HAIR TONIC. A bottle of this smelly purple mixture always stood on the shelf above the sink in the bathroom alongside all the toothbrushes, and a very vigorous scalp massage with OIL OF VIOLETS took place daily after shaving was completed. This hair and scalp massage was always accompanied by loud masculine grunts and heavy breathing and gasps of 'Ahhh, that's better! That's the stuff! Rub it right into the roots!' which could be clearly heard by Matilda in her bedroom across the corridor.

Now, in the early morning privacy of the bathroom, Matilda unscrewed the cap of her father's OIL OF VIOLETS and tipped three-quarters of the contents down the drain. Then she filled the bottle up with her mother's PLATINUM BLONDE HAIR-DYE EXTRA STRONG. She carefully left enough of her father's original hair tonic in the bottle so that when she gave it a good shake the whole thing still looked reasonably purple. She then replaced the bottle on the shelf above the sink, taking care to put her mother's bottle back in the cupboard. So far so good.

At breakfast time Matilda sat quietly at the dining-room table eating her cornflakes. Her brother sat opposite her with his back to the door devouring hunks of bread smothered with a mixture of peanut-butter and strawberry jam. The mother was just out of sight around the corner in the kitchen making Mr

Wormwood's breakfast which always had to be two fried eggs on fried bread with three pork sausages and three strips of bacon and some fried tomatoes.

At this point Mr Wormwood came noisily into the room. He was incapable of entering any room quietly, especially at breakfast time. He always had to make his appearance felt immediately by creating a lot of noise and clatter. One could almost hear him saying, 'It's me! Here I come, the great man himself, the master of the house, the wage-earner, the one who makes it possible for all the rest of you to live so well! Notice me and pay your respects!'

On this occasion he strode in and slapped his son on the back and shouted, 'Well, my boy, your father feels he's in for another great money-making day today at the garage! I've got a few little beauties I'm going to flog to the idiots this morning. Where's my breakfast?'

'It's coming, treasure,' Mrs Wormwood called from the kitchen.

Matilda kept her face bent low over her cornflakes. She didn't dare look up. In the first place she wasn't at all sure what she was going to see. And secondly, if she did see what she thought she was going to see, she wouldn't trust herself to keep a straight face. The son was looking directly ahead out of the window stuffing himself with bread and peanut-butter and strawberry jam.

The father was just moving round to sit at the head of the table when the mother came sweeping out from the kitchen carrying a huge plate piled high with eggs and sausages and bacon and tomatoes. She looked up. She caught sight of her husband. She stopped dead. Then she let out a scream that seemed to lift her right up into the air and she dropped the plate with a crash and a splash on to the floor. Everyone jumped, including Mr Wormwood.

'What the heck's the matter with you, woman?' he shouted. 'Look at the mess you've made on the carpet!'

'Your hair!' the mother was shrieking, pointing a quivering finger at her husband. 'Look at your *hair*! What've you done to your *hair*?'

'What's wrong with my hair, for heaven's sake?' he said.

'Oh my gawd, Dad, what've you done to your hair?' the son shouted.

A splendid noisy scene was building up nicely in the breakfast room.

Matilda said nothing. She simply sat there admiring the wonderful effect of her own handiwork. Mr Wormwood's fine crop of black hair was now a dirty silver, the colour this time of a tightrope-walker's tights that had not been washed for the entire circus season.

'You've . . . you've . . . you've *dyed* it!' shrieked the mother. 'Why did you do it, you fool! It looks absolutely frightful! It looks horrendous! You look like a freak!'

'What the blazes are you all talking about?' the father yelled, putting both hands to his hair. 'I most certainly have not dyed it! What d'you mean I've dyed it? What's happened to it? Or is this some sort of a stupid joke?' His face was turning pale green, the colour of sour apples.

'You must have dyed it, Dad,' the son said. 'It's the same colour as Mum's, only much dirtier-looking.'

'Of course he's dyed it!' the mother cried. 'It can't change colour all by itself! What on earth were you trying to do, make yourself look handsome or something? You look like someone's grandmother gone wrong!'

'Get me a mirror!' the father yelled. 'Don't just stand there shrieking at me! Get me a mirror!'

The mother's handbag lay on a chair at the other end of the table. She opened the bag and got out a powder compact that had a small round mirror on the inside of the lid. She opened the compact and handed it to her husband. He grabbed it and held it before his face and in doing so spilled most of the powder all over the front of his fancy tweed jacket.

'Be *careful*!' shrieked the mother. 'Now look what you've done! That's my best Elizabeth Arden face powder!'

'Oh my gawd!' yelled the father, staring into the little mirror. 'What's happened to me! I look terrible! I look just like *you* gone wrong! I can't go down to the garage and sell cars like this! How did it happen?' He stared round the room, first at the mother, then at the son, then at Matilda. 'How *could* it have happened?' he yelled.

'I imagine, Daddy,' Matilda said quietly, 'that you weren't looking very hard and you simply took Mummy's bottle of hair stuff off the shelf instead of your own.'

'Of *course* that's what happened!' the mother cried. 'Well really, Harry, how stupid can you get? Why didn't you read the label before you started splashing the stuff all over you! Mine's *terribly* strong. I'm only meant to use one tablespoon of it in a whole basin of water and you've gone and put it all over your head neat! It'll probably take all your hair off in the end! Is your scalp beginning to burn, dear?'

'You mean I'm going to lose all my hair?' the husband yelled.

'I think you will,' the mother said. 'Peroxide is a very powerful chemical. It's what they put down the lavatory to disinfect the pan, only they give it another name.'

'What are you saying!' the husband cried. 'I'm not a lavatory pan! I don't want to be disinfected!'

'Even diluted like I use it,' the mother told him, 'it makes a good deal of my hair fall out, so goodness knows what's going to happen to you. I'm surprised it didn't take the whole of the top of your head off!'

'What shall I do?' wailed the father. 'Tell me quick what to do before it starts falling out!'

Matilda said, 'I'd give it a good wash, Dad, if I were you, with soap and water. But you'll have to hurry.'

'Will that change the colour back?' the father asked anxiously.

'Of course it won't, you twit,' the mother said.

'Then what do I do? I can't go around looking like this for ever!'

'You'll have to have it dyed black,' the mother said. 'But wash it first or there won't be any there to dye.'

'Right!' the father shouted, springing into action. 'Get me an appointment with your hairdresser this instant for a hair-dyeing job! Tell them it's an emergency! They've got to boot someone else off their list! I'm going upstairs to wash it now!' With that the man dashed out of the room and Mrs Wormwood, sighing deeply, went to the telephone to call the beauty parlour.

'He does do some pretty silly things now and again, doesn't he, Mummy?' Matilda said.

The mother, dialling the number on the phone, said, 'I'm afraid men are not always quite as clever as they think they are. You will learn that when you get a bit older, my girl.'

But don't do that, do THIS!

# ★★ TRICK

## Surprise Shampoo

When Roald Dahl
wrote *Matilda*, he claimed that

*Oil of Violets Hair Tonic* and

### PLATINUM BLONDE HAIR-DYE EXTRA STRONG

could be found in every hairdresser and every barbershop around the world. Now, they're all gone. Every single bottle. Don't ask me why. As a writer he sometimes made things up. And don't panic either. For different hair effects, try adding these wonderful ingredients to the nearest shampoo bottle. Spectacular results are guaranteed.

★ ★ ★

What's the only kind of poo that doesn't smell horrible?
**Shampoo!**

⭐ Add two teaspoons of **GLITTER** for super-sparkly hair.

⭐ Add a few drops of **FOOD COLOURING** for red or yellow or green or blue or purple hair.

⭐ Or just fill an empty bottle with **CUSTARD**. When applied to hair, this yellow gloop will not make the hair glossy or shiny or sparkly or highlighted. It will not condition dry hair and it will not mean that the owner of long princess hair can swing it round their shoulders in a big curtain of loveliness as if they are starring in a television commercial. **It will just look as if a giant bird has pooped on their head.** And how funny would that be?

# Augustus Gloop Goes up the Pipe

*In which Augustus Gloop learns that drinking from a chocolate river is delicious yet VERY DANGEROUS.*

When Mr Wonka turned round and saw what Augustus Gloop was doing, he cried out, 'Oh, no! *Please*, Augustus, *please*! I beg of you not to do that. My chocolate must be untouched by human hands!'

'Augustus!' called out Mrs Gloop. 'Didn't you hear what the man said? Come away from that river at once!'

'This stuff is fabulous!' said Augustus, taking not the slightest notice of his mother or Mr Wonka. 'Gosh, I need a bucket to drink it properly!'

'Augustus,' cried Mr Wonka, hopping up and down and waggling his stick in the air, 'you *must* come away. You are dirtying my chocolate!'

'Augustus!' cried Mrs Gloop.

'Augustus!' cried Mr Gloop.

But Augustus was deaf to everything except the call of his enormous stomach. He was now lying full length on the ground with his head far out over the river, lapping up the chocolate like a dog.

'Augustus!' shouted Mrs Gloop. 'You'll be giving that nasty cold of yours to about a million people all over the country!'

'Be careful, Augustus!' shouted Mr Gloop. 'You're leaning too far out!'

Mr Gloop was absolutely right. For suddenly there was a shriek, and then a splash, and into the river went Augustus Gloop, and in one second he had disappeared under the brown surface.

'Save him!' screamed Mrs Gloop, going white in the face, and waving her umbrella about. 'He'll drown! He can't swim a yard! Save him! Save him!'

'Good heavens, woman,' said Mr Gloop, 'I'm not diving in there! I've got my best suit on!'

Augustus Gloop's face came up again to the surface,

painted brown with chocolate. 'Help! Help! Help!' he yelled. 'Fish me out!'

'Don't just *stand* there!' Mrs Gloop screamed at Mr Gloop. '*Do* something!'

'I *am* doing something!' said Mr Gloop, who was now taking off his jacket and getting ready to dive into the chocolate. But while he was doing this, the wretched boy was being sucked closer and closer towards the mouth of one of the great pipes that was dangling down into the river. Then all at once, the powerful suction took hold of him completely, and he was pulled under the surface and then into the mouth of the pipe.

The crowd on the riverbank waited breathlessly to see where he would come out.

'*There he goes!*' somebody shouted, pointing upwards.

And sure enough, because the pipe was made of glass, Augustus Gloop could be clearly seen shooting up inside it, head first, like a torpedo.

'Help! Murder! Police!' screamed Mrs Gloop. 'Augustus, come back at once! Where are you going?'

'It's a wonder to me,' said Mr Gloop, 'how that pipe is big enough for him to go through it.'

'It *isn't* big enough!' said Charlie Bucket. 'Oh dear, look! He's slowing down!'

'So he is!' said Grandpa Joe.

'He's going to stick!' said Charlie.

'I think he is!' said Grandpa Joe.

'By golly, he *has* stuck!' said Charlie.

'It's his stomach that's done it!' said Mr Gloop.

'He's blocked the whole pipe!' said Grandpa Joe.

'Smash the pipe!' yelled Mrs Gloop, still waving her umbrella. 'Augustus, come out of there at once!'

The watchers below could see the chocolate swishing around the boy in the pipe, and they could see it building up behind him in a solid mass, pushing against the blockage. The pressure was terrific. Something had to give. Something did give, and that something was Augustus. *WHOOF!* Up he shot again like a bullet in the barrel of a gun.

**But don't do that, do THIS!**

# ★★ TRiCK

# The Hot Chocolate That Isn't

**Everyone\*** loves chocolate. So why not take advantage of this fact and play a **FIENDISHLY** naughty trick on someone who simply adores the stuff?

*\*And if they don't, they clearly need a trip to a chocolate factory to sort them out.*

> What's the best thing to put into a chocolate pie? **Your teeth.**

## YOU WILL NEED:

☆ Two mugs

☆ Four teaspoons of drinking chocolate

☆ Two teaspoons of gravy mix

# WHAT YOU DO:

**1** Offer to make **hot chocolate** for an adult who loves chocolate.

**2** Make a mug of deliciously chocolatey hot chocolate using two teaspoons of drinking chocolate. (Ask an older person who's in on the trick to supervise the hot water or hot milk. You really don't want to spill it on yourself.)

**3** Make another mug of deliciously chocolatey hot chocolate using two teaspoons of drinking chocolate **AND two teaspoons of gravy mix**. Stir well.

**4** Now take the two drinks into the room where your unsuspecting adult is waiting.

**5** Give the mug of choco-gravy to the adult and (this is VERY important) keep the mug of real hot chocolate for yourself.

**6** Sip the hot chocolate and say, **'Mmmmmmmmmm...'**

**7** Wait for your victim to say, **'BLEURGHHHHHH!'**

# The Hat
## and the
## Superglue

*In which Matilda has decided to stand up for herself against her mean father by tampering with his pork-pie hat and sending him into an APOPLECTIC rage, all the while remaining so sweet and innocent that she cannot possibly be blamed.*

The hat itself was one of those flat-topped pork-pie jobs with a jay's feather stuck in the hatband and Mr Wormwood was very proud of it. He thought it gave him a rakish daring look, especially when he wore it at an angle with his loud checked jacket and green tie.

Matilda, holding the hat in one hand and a thin tube of Superglue in the other, proceeded to squeeze a line of glue very neatly all round the inside rim of the hat. Then she carefully hooked the hat back on to the peg with the walking-stick. She timed this operation very carefully, applying the glue just as her father was getting up from the breakfast table.

Mr Wormwood didn't notice anything when he put the hat on, but when he arrived at the garage he

couldn't get it off. Superglue is very powerful stuff, so powerful it will take your skin off if you pull too hard. Mr Wormwood didn't want to be scalped so he had to keep the hat on his head the whole day long, even when putting sawdust in gear-boxes and fiddling the mileages of cars with his electric drill. In an effort to save face, he adopted a casual attitude hoping that his staff would think that he actually meant to keep his hat on all day long just for the heck of it, like gangsters do in the films.

When he got home that evening he still couldn't get the hat off. 'Don't be silly,' his wife said. 'Come here. I'll take it off for you.'

She gave the hat a sharp yank. Mr Wormwood let out a yell that rattled the window-panes. 'Ow-w-w!' he screamed. 'Don't do that! Let go! You'll take half the skin off my forehead!'

Matilda, nestling in her usual chair, was watching this performance over the rim of her book with some interest.

'What's the matter, Daddy?' she said. 'Has your head suddenly swollen or something?'

The father glared at his daughter with deep suspicion, but said nothing. How could he? Mrs Wormwood said to him, 'It *must* be Superglue. It couldn't be anything else. That'll teach you to go playing around with nasty stuff like that. I expect you were trying to stick another feather in your hat.'

'I haven't touched the flaming stuff!' Mr Wormwood shouted. He turned and looked again at Matilda, who looked back at him with large innocent brown eyes.

Mrs Wormwood said to him, 'You should read the label on the tube before you start messing with dangerous products. Always follow the instructions on the label.'

'What in heaven's name are you talking about, you stupid witch?' Mr Wormwood shouted, clutching the brim of his hat to stop anyone trying to pull it off again. 'D'you think I'm so stupid I'd glue this thing to my head on purpose?'

Matilda said, 'There's a boy down the road who got some Superglue on his finger without knowing it and then he put his finger to his nose.'

Mr Wormwood jumped. 'What happened to him?' he spluttered.

'The finger got stuck inside his nose,' Matilda said, 'and he had to go around like that for a week. People kept saying to him, "Stop picking your nose," and he couldn't do anything about it. He looked an awful fool.'

'Serve him right,' Mrs Wormwood said. 'He shouldn't have put his finger up there in the first place. It's a nasty habit. If all children had Superglue put on their fingers they'd soon stop doing it.'

Matilda said, 'Grown-ups do it too, Mummy. I saw you doing it yesterday in the kitchen.'

'That's quite enough from you,' Mrs Wormwood said, turning pink.

Mr Wormwood had to keep his hat on all through supper in front of the television. He looked ridiculous and he stayed very silent.

When he went up to bed he tried again to get the thing off, and so did his wife, but it wouldn't budge. 'How am I going to have my shower?' he demanded.

'You'll just have to do without it, won't you,' his wife told him. And later on, as she watched her skinny little husband skulking around the bedroom in his purple-striped pyjamas with a pork-pie hat on his head, she thought how stupid he looked. Hardly the kind of man a wife dreams about, she told herself.

Mr Wormwood discovered that the worst thing about having a permanent hat on his head was having to sleep in it. It was impossible to lie comfortably on the pillow. 'Now do stop fussing around,' his wife said to him after he had been tossing and turning for about an hour. 'I expect it will be loose by the morning and then it'll slip off easily.'

But it wasn't loose by the morning and it wouldn't slip off. So Mrs Wormwood took a pair of scissors and cut the thing off his head, bit by bit, first the top and then the brim. Where the inner band had stuck to the hair all around the sides and back, she had to chop the hair off right to the skin so that he finished up with a bald white ring round his head, like some sort of a monk. And in the front, where the band had stuck directly to the bare skin, there remained a whole lot of small patches of brown leathery stuff that no amount

of washing would get off.

At breakfast Matilda said to him, 'You must try to get those bits off your forehead, Daddy. It looks as though you've got little brown insects crawling about all over you. People will think you've got lice.'

'Be quiet!' the father snapped. 'Just keep your nasty mouth shut, will you!'

All in all it was a most satisfactory exercise. But it was surely too much to hope that it had taught the father a permanent lesson.

But don't do that, do THIS!

# ★★★ TRICK

# Sticky Rocket

**Attention, please.** However mean and nasty someone has been, unless you are the heroine of a Roald Dahl story, it is best NOT to superglue someone's hat to their head. It would make the lovely doctors and nurses at the nearest hospital **VERY CROSS**. So, step away from the head of an actual human and step towards something truly **ASTRONOMICAL**.

## YOU WILL NEED:
☆ One rocket
☆ One launchpad
☆ 18 buckets (approx.) of industrial-grade superglue
☆ One spacesuit (with helmet)
☆ One tank of oxygen

# WHAT YOU DO:

**1** Go to your nearest **space centre**.
(There's a rather nice one at Cape Canaveral
in Florida, USA. You could go to a theme park while
you're there. Maybe visit the beach.)

**2** Locate the **launchpad** and wait for the dead of night.

**3** Carefully pour each of your **18 buckets of
industrial-grade superglue** on to the launchpad to
form a thin coating.

**4** **DO NOT STEP IN THE SUPERGLUE**.
(This is very important. You don't want to be glued to
the launchpad too.)

**5** Go back to your motel and wait until a **rocket** is
wheeled v-e-r-y s-l-o-w-l-y to the launchpad and
popped on top of it. You should hear a very sticky
**SLURP** when this happens.

**6** Go back to the space centre on launch day, **wearing
your spacesuit**. Don't forget your **oxygen tank** too.

**7** Count down with everyone else so that
**NO ONE SUSPECTS** your fiendishly clever plan.

**8** **Then . . . ta-daaaaa!** When the countdown
reaches zero, the rocket won't go ANYWHERE.*

* There is a slim chance that the rocket's engines will be so
megawattingly POWERFUL that it will shoot into space anyway and
take the launchpad, the surrounding tarmac and quite possibly YOU
with it, which is why you need the spacesuit and the oxygen too.
NEVER go to space without them.

# Spot the Mischief-maker

**Study the clues to identify one of Roald Dahl's STICKIEST, SWEETEST characters ever.**

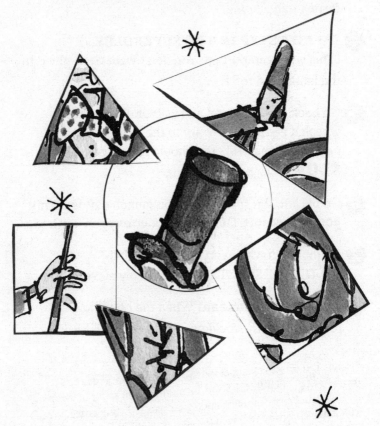

**1**

His voice is high and *flutey*. (Try talking in a high and flutey voice for a whole day. Your family will love it. Seriously.)

What kind of sweet is always late? **A chocolate.**

**2**

He wears a **black top hat**. He wears a **tail coat** made of beautiful plum-coloured velvet. His **trousers** are bottle green. His **gloves** are pearly grey. (Goodness, how smart!)

**3**

He's like a quick **clever old squirrel** from the park. (Except he's NOT a squirrel. But he does employ squirrels . . .)

**4**

He can make rich caramels that change colour every ten seconds as you suck them. (Mmm . . .)

**5**

He once built a colossal palace entirely out of **CHOCOLATE**. The bricks were chocolate, and the cement holding them together was chocolate, and the windows were chocolate and all the walls and ceilings were made of chocolate, so were the carpets and the pictures and the furniture and the beds; and when you turned on the taps in the bathroom hot chocolate came pouring out.

# Who is he?

The answer is on page 164.

# Gooey Questions

**Congratulations!** You've NEARLY reached the end of the first chapter. All you have to do is answer these icky, sticky, super-tricky questions about **GOO** and then you're done.

But be warned: they are for Roald Dahl Experts only.

 **1** Inside which type of chocolate bar did **Charlie** find a Golden Ticket?

 **2** Who did **Willy Wonka** build a chocolate palace for?

 **3** What did **George** add to make his marvellous medicine brown?

 **4** How did **Mr Twit** catch the birds for his Bird Pie?

The answers are on page 165. If you got all four correct, cartwheel around your nearest supermarket. If you didn't, go for a ride on a fuzzy fruit with a squidgy worm inside … or read *James and the Giant Peach* again. Whichever's easier.

From Boy

# The Matron

*In which Roald Dahl's school friend Wragg makes
Matron go CRUNCH, CRUNCH, CRUNCH and
then GRR, GRR, GRRRRRRR.*

After 'lights out' the Matron would prowl the corridor
like a panther trying to catch the sound of a whisper
behind a dormitory door, and we soon learnt that her
powers of hearing were so phenomenal that it was
safer to keep quiet.

Once, after lights out, a brave boy called Wragg
tiptoed out of our dormitory and sprinkled caster
sugar all over the linoleum floor of the corridor. When
Wragg returned and told us that the corridor had
been successfully sugared from one end to the other,
I began shivering with excitement. I lay there in the
dark in my bed waiting and waiting for the Matron to
go on the prowl. Nothing happened. Perhaps, I told
myself, she is in her room taking another speck of dust

out of Mr Victor Corrado's eye.

Suddenly, from far down the corridor came a resounding *crunch*! *Crunch crunch crunch* went the footsteps. It sounded as though a giant was walking on loose gravel.

Then we heard the high-pitched furious voice of the Matron in the distance. 'Who did this?' she was shrieking. 'How *dare* you do this!' She went crunching along the corridor flinging open all the dormitory doors and switching on all the lights. The intensity of her fury was frightening. 'Come along!' she cried out, marching with crunching steps up and down the corridor. 'Own up! I want the name of the filthy little boy who put down the sugar! Own up immediately! Step forward! Confess!'

'Don't own up,' we whispered to Wragg. 'We won't give you away!'

Wragg kept quiet. I didn't blame him for that. Had he owned up, it was certain his fate would have been a terrible and a bloody one.

Soon the Headmaster was summoned from below. The Matron, with steam coming out of her nostrils, cried out to him for help and now the whole school was herded into the long corridor, where we stood freezing in our pyjamas and bare feet while the culprit or culprits were ordered to step forward.

Nobody stepped forward.

I could see that the Headmaster was getting very angry indeed. His evening had been interrupted. Red splotches were appearing all over his face and flecks of spit were shooting out of his mouth as he talked.

'Very well!' he thundered. 'Every one of you will go at once and get the key to his tuck-box! Hand the keys to Matron, who will keep them for the rest of the term! And all parcels coming from home will be confiscated from now on! I will not tolerate this kind of behaviour!'

We handed in our keys and throughout the remaining six weeks of the term we went very hungry.

**But don't do that, do THIS!**

# TRICK

## The Really-Sweet Trick

**Why not try the Super Fine Sugar Trick for yourself?**
It's so cunning that it is rumoured **top-secret spies** use the
technique to predict when baddies are approaching. But if you're
going to do it at home remember these three simple rules:

**1** **Never sprinkle sugar on a carpet.** It must be a hard
floor, always.

**2** **The bigger the grains of sugar, the louder the
crunch.** If you really want to make people sit up and
listen, go for muscovado or Demerara. But for a crunch
so gentle that it just tickles the edge of the sugar-
cruncher's hearing, making them wonder if they've
heard it at all, do as Wragg did and go for superfine
sugar. Then you can use the rest to make a cake.

**3** **Learn how to use a vacuum cleaner before you
start.** Because there's a fairly big chance you will have
to use it afterwards.

# From The Wonderful Story of Henry Sugar

*In which Henry Sugar develops his X-ray vision and learns to see THROUGH playing cards and read what's on the other side. This means that he's very, very, very, very (now, imagine another 258 verys because he's that good and there isn't room on this page to write them all down) good at playing card games – and winning them.*

Some time during the tenth month, Henry became aware, just as Imhrat Khan had done before him, of a slight ability to see an object with his eyes closed. When he closed his eyes and stared at something hard, with fierce concentration, he could actually see the outline of the object he was looking at.

'It's coming to me!' he cried. 'I'm doing it! It's fantastic!'

Now he worked harder than ever at his exercises with the candle, and at the end of the first year he could actually concentrate upon the image of his own face for no less than five and a half minutes!

At this point, he decided the time had come to test himself with the cards. He was in the living-room of his London flat when he made this decision and it was near midnight. He got out a pack of cards and a pencil and paper. He was shaking with excitement. He placed the pack upside down before him and concentrated on the top card.

All he could see at first was the design on the back of the card. It was a very ordinary design of thin red lines, one of the commonest playing-card designs in the world. He now shifted his concentration from the pattern itself to the other side of the card. He concentrated with great intensity upon the invisible underneath of the card, and he allowed no other single thought to creep into his mind. Thirty seconds went by.

Then one minute . . .

Two minutes . . .

Three minutes . . .

Henry didn't move. His concentration was intense and absolute. He was visualizing the reverse side of the playing-card. No other thought of any kind was allowed to enter his head.

During the fourth minute, something began to happen. Slowly, magically, but very clearly, the black symbols became spades and alongside the spades appeared the figure five.

The five of spades!

Henry switched off his concentration. And now, with shaking fingers, he picked up the card and turned it over.

It *was* the five of spades!

'I've done it!' he cried aloud, leaping up from his chair. 'I've seen through it! I'm on my way!'

But don't do that, do THIS!

# ★ TRICK

## A Quick Card Trick

**If you have X-RAY VISION like Henry Sugar, GREAT.** You're probably already very good at playing card games – and winning them. If not, never mind. Ten months is an awfully long time to spend learning how to do it. And it would be very awkward explaining to teachers why you don't have time to do any homework.

**For more instant results:**

 Simply place other card players in front of a large shiny surface. **A mirror is PERFECT**.

Then just look in the mirror and you'll be able to see the **other side of their cards reflected** there.

 You'll have to **learn how to read backwards**, obviously. But that's a bit simpler than learning how to see through solid objects.

# Capture

*In which Sophie is VERY BRAVE and, with
the help of the BFG, tackles a VERY BIG and
VERY UNFRIENDLY giant.*

Sophie ran up behind the Fleshlumpeater. She was
holding the brooch between her fingers. When she
was right up close to the great naked hairy legs, she
rammed the three-inch-long pin of the brooch as
hard as she could into the Fleshlumpeater's right
ankle. It went deep into the flesh
and stayed there.

The giant gave
a roar of pain and
jumped high in the
air. He dropped
the soldier and
made a grab for
his ankle.

The BFG, knowing what a coward the Fleshlumpeater was, saw his chance. 'You is bitten by a snake!' he shouted. 'I seed it biting you! It was a frightsome poisnowse viper! It was a dreadly dungerous vindscreen viper!'

'Save our souls!' bellowed the Fleshlumpeater. 'Sound the crumpets! I is bitten by a septicous venomsome vindscreen viper!' He flopped to the ground and sat there howling his head off and clutching his ankle with both hands. His fingers felt the brooch. 'The teeth of the dreadly viper is still sticking into me!' he yelled. 'I is feeling the teeth sticking into my anklet!'

The BFG saw his second chance. 'We must be getting those viper's teeth out at once!' he cried. 'Otherwise you is deader than duck-soup! I is helping you!'

The BFG knelt down beside the Fleshlumpeater. 'You must grab your anklet very tight with both hands!' he ordered. 'That will stop the poisnowse juices from the venomsome viper going up your leg and into your heart!'

The Fleshlumpeater grabbed his ankle with both hands.

'Now close your eyes and grittle your teeth and look up to heaven and say your prayers while I is taking out the teeth of the venomsome viper,' the BFG said.

The terrified Fleshlumpeater did exactly as he was told.

The BFG signalled for some rope. A soldier rushed

it over to him. With both the Fleshlumpeater's hands
gripping his ankle, it was a simple matter for the BFG
to tie the ankles and hands together with a tight knot.

'I is pulling out the frightsome viper's teeth!' the
BFG said as he pulled the knot tight.

'Do it quickly!' shouted the Fleshlumpeater, 'before
I is pizzened to death!'

'There we is,' said the BFG, standing up. 'You can
look now.'

When the Fleshlumpeater saw that he was trussed
up like a turkey, he gave a yell so loud that the heavens
trembled. He rolled and he wriggled, he fought and

he figgled, he squirmed and he squiggled. But there was not a thing he could do.

'Well done you!' Sophie cried.

'Well done *you*!' said the BFG, smiling down at the little girl. 'You is saving all of our lives!'

'Will you please get that brooch back for me,' Sophie said. 'It belongs to the Queen.'

But don't do that, do THIS!

# ★★ TRICK

## Four Ways to Trick a Giant

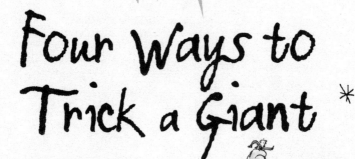

Unless you live in a land of thick forests and rushing rivers and hills as bare as concrete and ground that is flat and pale yellow, with great lumps of blue rock scattered around and dead trees standing around like skeletons – which is the land where the **BFG** lives – then you are unlikely to meet a real live **giant**. So the next biggest thing is a really tall grown-up. Trick one of those instead!

**1** **Take the batteries out of the TV remote control.** Hide them. Replace the remote control. Now it will be more entertaining watching the grown-up trying to make the TV work than the TV itself! (For an even better trick, secretly replace the batteries and then tell the grown-up that they must have been doing it wrong, because – look! – the remote control is working **PERFECTLY**.)

**2** **Stuff newspaper inside shoes.** Make sure it's right down at the toes so the grown-up doesn't see it before they put their feet in. Fill **ALL** shoes and boots, even ones that the grown-up hardly ever wears, for fun **ALL THROUGH THE YEAR.** How they'll laugh!

**3** **Change the time on the clocks.** All of the clocks. Get up really early one morning and move them an hour forward. Then **EVERYONE** will be an hour early for work and school. Except you. You can have a lie-in. **Bwa-ha-haaa!**

**4** **Press the volume button on the TV remote control** to the loudest it will go when it is turned off. The next person who turns on the TV will have the **FRIGHT OF HIS OR HER LIFE!**

When is a magician in a car not a magician in a car? **When he turns into a driveway.**

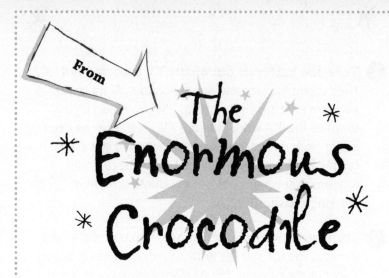

From

# The Enormous Crocodile

*In which the Enormous Crocodile creates the world's best fancy-dress outfit EVER.*

The Enormous Crocodile crept over to a place where there were a lot of coconut trees.

He knew that children from the town often came here looking for coconuts. The trees were too tall for them to climb, but there were always some coconuts on the ground that had fallen down.

The Enormous Crocodile quickly collected all the coconuts that were lying on the ground. He also gathered together several fallen branches.

'Now for Clever Trick Number One!' he whispered to himself. 'It won't be long before I am eating the first part of my lunch!'

He took all the coconut branches and held them between his teeth.

He grasped the coconuts in his front paws. Then he stood straight up in the air, balancing himself on his tail.

He arranged the branches and the coconuts so cleverly that he now looked exactly like a small coconut tree standing among the big coconut trees.

Soon, two children came along. They were brother and sister. The boy was called Toto. His sister was called Mary. They walked around looking for fallen coconuts, but they couldn't find any because the Enormous Crocodile had gathered them all up.

'Oh look!' cried Toto. 'That tree over there is much smaller than the others! And it's full of coconuts! I think I could climb that one quite easily if you help me up the first bit.'

Toto and Mary ran towards what they thought was the small coconut tree.

The Enormous Crocodile peered through the branches, watching them as they came closer and closer. He licked his lips. He began to dribble with excitement.

Suddenly there was a tremendous whooshing noise. It was Humpy-Rumpy, the Hippopotamus. He came crashing and snorting out of the jungle. His head was down low and he was galloping at a terrific speed.

'Look out, Toto!' shouted Humpy-Rumpy. 'Look out, Mary! That's not a coconut tree! It's the Enormous Crocodile and he wants to eat you up!'

But don't do that, do THIS!

# ★★★ TRICK

## How to Disguise Yourself as a Coconut Tree

Don't be put off by the three stars. This really is a very simple trick, as long as you have the following everyday items to hand.

**YOU WILL NEED:**
- ☆ One speedboat (but don't worry if you haven't got a speedboat – a helicopter will do just fine)
- ☆ One desert island
- ☆ 54 yards of coconut matting
- ☆ 34 coconut leaves
- ☆ One helper

## WHAT YOU DO:

**1** Travel to the desert island by **speedboat** or **helicopter**.

**2** Ask your helper to **roll you up in the coconut matting**, but make sure your head is poking out of the top. Otherwise, it could get a bit boring in there.

**3** Ask your helper to stick the **34 coconut leaves** at the top of the matting, so that they sprout outwards like A REAL TREE, while cunningly hiding your head at the same time.

**4** **There. You're done.**

**5** Um . . . watch helplessly as your helper escapes from the desert island in the speedboat or the helicopter and leaves you stranded there.

**6** **Cheer up!** That's a fabulous outfit. You look JUST LIKE a coconut tree. **Bravo!**

# Spot the Mischief-maker

**Can you work out which Roald Dahl character this is?**

**1** He is clever. How clever? Probably cleverer than all of your teachers at school and **Newton** and **Einstein** and **Professor Stephen Hawking** put together. THAT clever. And then some.

What do you say to a magician with white rabbits in his ears? **Anything you like – he can't hear you.**

**2** He has a long handsome face.

**3** He has had the finest tail for miles around, until . . . Well, THAT would be giving the game away.

**4** He doesn't like farmers, especially not **Farmer Boggis**, **Farmer Bunce** and **Farmer Bean**. And you wouldn't either if you knew them.

**5** He is **FANTASTIC**. (Have you got it yet? Have you? HAVE YOU? Because this is officially the Biggest Clue Ever.)

# Who is he?

The answer is on page 164.

# Terrible Tricks

**Phew!** You must be exhausted after so much trickery. Grab a glass of that refreshing fizzy stuff that rots your teeth. (I'm sure your dentist will love the extra business.) Now put your feet up and relax with this **FEARSOME QUIZ**. Can you spot the victim of Willy Wonka's four best tricks?

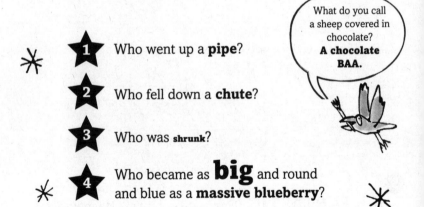

What do you call a sheep covered in chocolate?
**A chocolate BAA.**

**1** Who went up a **pipe**?

**2** Who fell down a **chute**?

**3** Who was shrunk?

**4** Who became as **big** and round and blue as a **massive blueberry**?

The answers are on page 165. If you got all four correct, perform a celebratory rumba. If you didn't, read *Charlie and the Chocolate Factory* again. It really is terribly good.

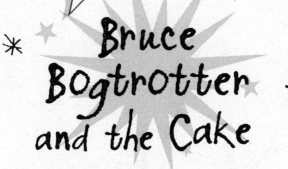

# Bruce Bogtrotter and the Cake

*In which Bruce Bogtrotter shows a great deal of chocolate-based bravery.*

There was a small table centre stage with a chair behind it. The cook placed the cake carefully on the table. 'Sit down, Bogtrotter,' the Trunchbull said. 'Sit there.'

The boy moved cautiously to the table and sat down. He stared at the gigantic cake.

'There you are, Bogtrotter,' the Trunchbull said, and once again her voice became soft, persuasive, even gentle. 'It's all for you, every bit of it. As you enjoyed that slice you had yesterday so very much, I ordered cook to bake you an extra large one all for yourself.'

'Well, thank you,' the boy said, totally bemused.

'Thank cook, not me,' the Trunchbull said.

'Thank you, cook,' the boy said.

The cook stood there like a shrivelled bootlace, tight-lipped, implacable, disapproving. She looked as though her mouth was full of lemon juice.

'Come on then,' the Trunchbull said. 'Why don't you cut yourself a nice thick slice and try it?'

'What? Now?' the boy said, cautious. He knew there was a catch in this somewhere, but he wasn't sure where. 'Can't I take it home instead?' he asked.

'That would be impolite,' the Trunchbull said, with a crafty grin. 'You must show cookie here how grateful you are for all the trouble she's taken.'

The boy didn't move.

'Go on, get on with it,' the Trunchbull said. 'Cut a slice and taste it. We haven't got all day.'

The boy picked up the knife and was about to cut into the cake when he stopped. He stared at the cake. Then he looked up at the Trunchbull, then at the tall stringy cook with her lemon-juice mouth. All the children in the hall were watching tensely, waiting for something to happen. They felt certain it must. The Trunchbull was not a person who would give someone a whole chocolate cake to eat just out of kindness. Many were guessing that it had been filled with pepper or castor-oil or some other foul-tasting substance that would make the boy violently sick. It might even be arsenic and he would be dead in ten seconds flat. Or perhaps it was a booby-trapped cake and the whole thing would blow up the moment it was cut, taking Bruce Bogtrotter with it. No one in the school put it past the Trunchbull to do any of these things.

'I don't want to eat it,' the boy said.

'Taste it, you little brat,' the Trunchbull said. 'You're insulting the cook.'

Very gingerly the boy began to cut a thin slice of the vast cake. Then he levered the slice out. Then he put down the knife and took the sticky thing in his fingers and started very slowly to eat it.

'It's good, isn't it?' the Trunchbull asked.

'Very good,' the boy said, chewing and swallowing. He finished the slice.

'Have another,' the Trunchbull said.

'That's enough, thank you,' the boy murmured.

'I said have another,' the Trunchbull said, and now there was an altogether sharper edge to her voice. 'Eat another slice! Do as you are told!'

'I don't want another slice,' the boy said.

Suddenly the Trunchbull exploded. 'Eat!' she

shouted, banging her thigh with the riding-crop. 'If I tell you to eat, you will eat! You wanted cake! You stole cake! And now you've got cake! What's more, you're going to eat it! You do not leave this platform and nobody leaves this hall until you have eaten the entire cake that is sitting there in front of you! Do I make myself clear, Bogtrotter? Do you get my meaning?'

The boy looked at the Trunchbull. Then he looked down at the enormous cake.

'Eat! Eat! Eat!' the Trunchbull was yelling.

Very slowly the boy cut himself another slice and began to eat it.

Matilda was fascinated. 'Do you think he can do it?' she whispered to Lavender.

'No,' Lavender whispered back. 'It's impossible. He'd be sick before he was halfway through.'

The boy kept going. When he had finished the second slice, he looked at the Trunchbull, hesitating.

'Eat!' she shouted. 'Greedy little thieves who like to eat cake must have cake! Eat faster boy! Eat faster! We don't want to be here all day! And don't stop like you're doing now! Next time you stop before it's all finished you'll go straight into The Chokey and I shall lock the door and throw the key down the well!'

The boy cut a third slice and started to eat it. He finished this one quicker than the other two and when that was done he immediately picked up the knife and cut the next slice. In some peculiar way he seemed to be getting into his stride.

Matilda, watching closely, saw no signs of distress

in the boy yet. If anything, he seemed to be gathering confidence as he went along. 'He's doing well,' she whispered to Lavender.

'He'll be sick soon,' Lavender whispered back. 'It's going to be horrid.'

When Bruce Bogtrotter had eaten his way through half of the entire enormous cake, he paused for just a couple of seconds and took several deep breaths.

The Trunchbull stood with hands on hips, glaring at him. 'Get on with it!' she shouted. 'Eat it up!'

Suddenly the boy let out a gigantic belch which rolled around the Assembly Hall like thunder. Many of the audience began to giggle.

'Silence!' shouted the Trunchbull.

The boy cut himself another thick slice and started eating it fast. There were still no signs of flagging or

giving up. He certainly did not look as though he was about to stop and cry out, 'I can't, I can't eat any more! I'm going to be sick!' He was still in there running.

And now a subtle change was coming over the two hundred and fifty watching children in the audience. Earlier on, they had sensed impending disaster. They had prepared themselves for an unpleasant scene in which the wretched boy, stuffed to the gills with chocolate cake, would have to surrender and beg for mercy and then they would have watched the triumphant Trunchbull forcing more and still more cake into the mouth of the gasping boy.

Not a bit of it. Bruce Bogtrotter was three-quarters of the way through and still going strong. One sensed that he was almost beginning to enjoy himself. He had a mountain to climb and he was jolly well going to reach the top or die in the attempt. What is more, he had now become very conscious of his audience and of how they were all silently rooting for him. This was nothing less than a battle between him and the mighty Trunchbull.

Suddenly someone shouted, 'Come on, Brucie! You can make it!'

The Trunchbull wheeled round and yelled, 'Silence!' The audience watched intently. They were thoroughly caught up in the contest. They were longing to start cheering but they didn't dare.

'I think he's going to make it,' Matilda whispered.

'I think so too,' Lavender whispered back. 'I wouldn't have believed anyone in the world could eat the whole of a cake that size.'

'The Trunchbull doesn't believe it either,' Matilda whispered. 'Look at her. She's turning redder and redder. She's going to kill him if he wins.'

The boy was slowing down now. There was no doubt about that. But he kept pushing the stuff into his mouth with the dogged perseverance of a long-distance runner who has sighted the finishing-line and knows he must keep going. As the very last mouthful disappeared, a tremendous cheer rose up from the audience, and children were leaping on to their chairs and yelling and clapping and shouting, 'Well done, Brucie! Good for you, Brucie! You've won a gold medal, Brucie!'

The Trunchbull stood motionless on the platform. Her great horsy face had turned the colour of molten lava and her eyes were glittering with fury. She glared at Bruce Bogtrotter, who was sitting on his chair like some huge overstuffed grub, replete, comatose, unable to move or to speak. A fine sweat was beading his forehead but there was a grin of triumph on his face.

Suddenly the Trunchbull lunged forward and grabbed the large empty china platter on which the cake had rested. She raised it high in the air and brought it down with a crash right on the top of the wretched Bruce Bogtrotter's head and pieces flew all over the platform.

The boy was by now so full of cake he was like a sackful of wet cement and you couldn't have hurt him with a sledge-hammer. He simply shook his head a few times and went on grinning.

'Go to blazes!' screamed the Trunchbull and she marched off the platform followed closely by the cook.

**But don't do that, do THIS!**

# ☆ TRICK

This is not a trick but a very scientific chocolate-based experiment, because **EVERYONE** needs a break from mischief now and again.

# TODAY, READER, YOU ARE
# BRUCE BOGTROTTER.

Go on, admit it. You've always wondered what it would be like to be Bruce Bogtrotter, haven't you? I bet, deep down, you think that **YOU** could eat that **enormous chocolate cake** too. And in probably half the time. So make your own chocolate cake and **EAT IT ALL**.*

* Or if adults throw up their hands in horror and start screeching about calorific content and other REALLY DULL nutritional stuff and threatening you with healthy steamed vegetables, then invite a few friends to your home and make a dinner party of it instead. (At least that way you won't be sick.)

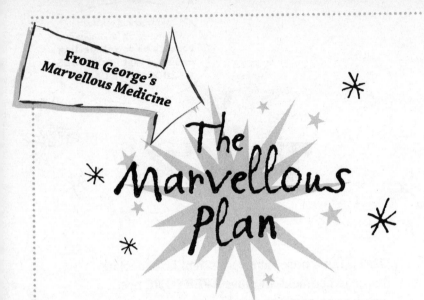

# The Marvellous Plan

*In which George decides to make his very own magic medicine to treat his horrid grandma.*

George sat himself down at the table in the kitchen. He was shaking a little. Oh, how he hated Grandma! He really *hated* that horrid old witchy woman. And all of a sudden he had a tremendous urge to *do something* about her. Something *whopping*. Something *absolutely terrific*. A *real shocker*. A sort of explosion. He wanted to blow away the witchy smell that hung about her in the next room. He may have been only eight years old but he was a brave little boy. He was ready to take this old woman on.

'I'm not going to be frightened by *her*,' he said softly to himself. But he *was* frightened. And that's why he wanted suddenly to explode her away.

Well . . . not quite away. But he did want to shake the old woman up a bit.

Very well, then. What should it be, this whopping terrific exploding shocker for Grandma?

He would have liked to put a firework banger under her chair but he didn't have one.

He would have liked to put a long green snake down the back of her dress but he didn't have a long green snake.

He would have liked to put six big black rats in the room with her and lock the door but he didn't have six big black rats.

As George sat there pondering this interesting problem, his eye fell upon the bottle of Grandma's brown medicine standing on the sideboard. Rotten stuff it seemed to be. Four times a day a large spoonful of it was shovelled into her mouth and it didn't do her the slightest bit of good. She was always just as horrid after she'd had it as she'd been before.

The whole point of medicine, surely, was to make a person better. If it didn't do that, then it was quite useless.

*So-ho!* thought George suddenly. *Ah-ha! Hohum!* I know exactly what I'll do. I shall make her a *new* medicine, one that is so strong and so fierce and so fantastic it will either cure her completely or blow off the top of her head. I'll make her a *magic medicine*, a medicine no doctor in the world has ever made before.

George looked at the kitchen clock. It said five past ten. There was nearly an hour left before Grandma's next dose was due at eleven.

'Here we go, then!' cried George, jumping up from the table. 'A magic medicine it shall be!'

'So give me a bug and a jumping flea,
Give me two snails and lizards three,
And a slimy squiggler from the sea,
And the poisonous sting of a bumblebee,
And the juice from the fruit of the ju-jube
    tree,
And the powdered bone of a wombat's
    knee.
And one hundred other things as well
Each with a rather nasty smell.

I'll stir them up, I'll boil them long,
A mixture tough, a mixture strong.
And then, heigh-ho, and down it goes,
A nice big spoonful (hold your nose)
Just gulp it down and have no fear.
"How do you like it, Granny dear?"
Will she go pop? Will she explode?
Will she go flying down the road?
Will she go poof in a puff of smoke?
Start fizzing like a can of Coke?
Who knows? Not I. Let's wait and see.
(I'm glad it's neither you nor me.)
Oh Grandma, if you only knew
What I have got in store for you!'

But don't do that, do THIS!

# ★★ TRICK

# A Recipe for Chocolate and Brussels Sprout Pie

It's a well-known fact that grown-ups adore eating vegetables nearly as much as they adore making younger people eat vegetables. So they are bound to LOVE this delightful pie. Why not rustle one up at the weekend, feed it to the grown-ups of your choice and THEN get them to guess what's in it?

> PS If they make lots of weird noises like **BLEURGH** and **EEUCH**, tell them that it's good for them and not to whine. Just like they tell you.

## YOU WILL NEED:

☆ One spoonful of butter or margarine or posh spread made from olives

☆ One pie dish

☆ One rolling pin

☆ One packet of puff pastry

☆ One bag of Brussels sprouts

☆ One bar of very dark chocolate

☆ One egg

☆ One oven

☆ One group of grown-ups, preferably the healthy sort

**OPTIONAL INGREDIENTS:**
Cabbage, Marmite, chocolate sprinkles, syrup, baked beans, puréed pumpkin, jam, tinned carrots and sardines. Mmm.

# WHAT YOU DO:

**1** **Rub** the butter, margarine or posh spread made from olives into your pie dish.

**2** **Roll out two circles of pastry.** Put one of them into your pie dish.

**3** Put the **Brussels sprouts** into the pie dish.

**4** Break the **chocolate** up into squares and put that in too.

**5** Add as many of the optional ingredients as you like.

**6** Place the other circle of pastry on top of the pie dish and **seal the pastry round the edges** by pinching them together.

**7** **Paint the top of the pie** with beaten egg, just to make it look super appetizing when it's cooked.

**8** **Ask an adult to help you pop it in the oven.** Bake for 45 minutes to an hour at 375° F or moderate oven.

# Goat's Tobacco

*In which Roald Dahl swaps tobacco for something EVEN SMELLIER.*

One day, we all went in our little motor-boat to an island we had never been to before, and for once the ancient half-sister and the manly lover decided to come with us. We chose this particular island because we saw some goats on it. They were climbing about on the rocks and we thought it would be fun to go and visit them. But when we landed, we found that the goats were totally wild and we couldn't get near them. So we gave up trying to make friends with them and simply sat around on the smooth rocks in our bathing costumes, enjoying the lovely sun.

The manly lover was filling his pipe. I happened to be watching him as he very carefully packed the tobacco into the bowl from a yellow oilskin pouch. He had just finished doing this and was about to light up when the ancient half-sister called on him to come swimming. So he put down the pipe and off he went.

I stared at the pipe that was lying there on the rocks. About twelve inches away from it, I saw a little heap of dried goat's droppings, each one small and round like a pale brown berry, and at that point, an interesting idea began to sprout in my mind. I picked up the pipe and knocked all the tobacco out of it. I then took the goat's droppings and teased them with my fingers until they were nicely shredded. Very gently I poured these shredded droppings into the bowl of the pipe, packing them down with my thumb just as the manly lover always did it. When that was done, I placed a thin layer of real tobacco over the top. The entire family was watching me as I did this. Nobody said a word, but I could sense a glow of approval all round. I replaced the pipe on the rock, and all of us sat back to await the return of the victim. The whole lot of us were in this together now, even my mother. I had drawn them into the plot simply by letting them see what I was doing. It was a silent, rather dangerous family conspiracy.

Back came the manly lover, dripping wet from the sea, chest out, strong and virile, healthy and sunburnt. 'Great swim!' he announced to the world. 'Splendid water! Terrific stuff!' He towelled himself vigorously, making the muscles of his biceps ripple, then he sat down on the rocks and reached for his pipe.

Nine pairs of eyes watched him intently. Nobody giggled to give the game away. We were trembling with anticipation, and a good deal of the suspense was caused by the fact that none of us knew just what was going to happen.

The manly lover put the pipe between his strong white teeth and struck a match. He held the flame over the bowl and sucked. The tobacco ignited and glowed, and the lover's head was enveloped in clouds of blue smoke. 'Ah-h-h,' he said, blowing smoke through his nostrils. 'There's nothing like a good pipe after a bracing swim.'

Still we waited. We could hardly bear the suspense. The sister who was seven couldn't bear it at all. 'What *sort* of tobacco do you put in that thing?' she asked with superb innocence.

'Navy Cut,' the male lover answered. 'Player's Navy Cut. It's the best there is. These Norwegians use all sorts of disgusting scented tobaccos, but I wouldn't touch them.'

'I didn't know they had different tastes,' the small sister went on.

'Of course they do,' the manly lover said. 'All tobaccos are different to the discriminating pipe-smoker. Navy Cut is clean and unadulterated. It's a man's smoke.' The man seemed to go out of his way to use long words like discriminating and unadulterated. We hadn't the foggiest what they meant.

The ancient half-sister, fresh from her swim and now clothed in a towel bathrobe, came and sat herself

close to her manly lover. Then the two of them
started giving each other those silly little glances and
soppy smiles that made us all feel sick. They were far
too occupied with one another to notice the awful
tension that had settled over our group. They didn't
even notice that every face in the crowd was turned
towards them. They had sunk once again into their
lovers' world where little children did not exist.

The sea was calm, the sun was shining and it was
a beautiful day.

Then all of a sudden, the manly lover let out a
piercing scream and his whole body shot about four
feet into the air. His pipe flew out of his mouth and
went clattering over the rocks, and the second scream
he gave was so shrill and loud that all the seagulls on
the island rose up in alarm. His features were twisted
like those of a person undergoing severe torture, and

his skin had turned the colour of snow. He began spluttering and choking and spewing and hawking and acting generally like a man with some serious internal injury. He was completely speechless.

We stared at him, enthralled.

The ancient half-sister, who must have thought she was about to lose her future husband for ever, was pawing at him and thumping him on the back and crying, 'Darling! Darling! What's happening to you? Where does it hurt? Get the boat! Start the engine! We must rush him to a hospital quickly!' She seemed to have forgotten that there wasn't a hospital within fifty miles.

'I've been poisoned!' spluttered the manly lover. 'It's got into my lungs! It's in my chest! My chest is on fire! My stomach's going up in flames!'

'Help me get him into the boat! Quick!' cried the ancient half-sister, gripping him under the armpits. 'Don't just sit there staring! Come and help!'

'No, no, no!' cried the now not-so-manly lover. 'Leave me alone! I need air! Give me air!' He lay back and breathed in deep draughts of splendid Norwegian ocean air, and in another minute or so, he was sitting up again and was on the way to recovery.

'What in the world came over you?' asked the ancient half-sister, clasping his hands tenderly in hers.

'I can't imagine,' he murmured. 'I simply can't imagine.' His face was as still and white as virgin snow and his hands were trembling. 'There must be a reason for it,' he added. 'There's got to be a reason.'

'I know the reason!' shouted the seven-year-old sister, screaming with laughter. 'I know what it was!'

'What was it?' snapped the ancient one. 'What have you been up to? Tell me at once!'

'It's his pipe!' shouted the small sister, still convulsed with laughter.

'What's wrong with my pipe?' said the manly lover.

'You've been smoking goat's tobacco!' cried the small sister.

It took a few moments for the full meaning of these words to dawn upon the two lovers, but when it did, and when the terrible anger began to show itself on the manly lover's face, and when he started to rise slowly and menacingly to his feet, we all sprang up and ran for our lives and jumped off the rocks into the deep water.

But don't do that, do THIS!

# ★★ TRiCK
## Super Poop

You don't have to grub about collecting **goat's poop** like Roald Dahl did. (Well, you can if you want to, but make sure you wash your hands afterwards.) It's much more fun using . . .

## FAKE POOP.

**Chocolate-covered raisins** are perfect. Scatter these around the house and tell everyone they are mouse or squirrel or small donkey droppings. And if you really want to shock your audience pick one up, pop it in your mouth and declare it to be **'DELICIOUS'.***

* Stand by to catch any great-aunts. This is the sort of thing that might make them faint with horror.

From Boy

# Corkers

*In which Roald Dahl's maths teacher – Corkers – claims that he can smell a very stinky stink and blames his TOTALLY INNOCENT pupils.*

He would be talking to us about this or that when suddenly he would stop in mid-sentence and a look of intense pain would cloud his ancient countenance. Then his head would come up and his great nose would begin to sniff the air and he would cry aloud, 'By God! This is too much! This is going too far! This is intolerable!'

We knew exactly what was coming next, but we always played along with him. 'What's the matter, sir? What's happened? Are you all right, sir? Are you feeling ill?'

Up went the great nose once again, and the head would move slowly from side to side and the nose would sniff the air delicately as though searching for a leak of gas or the smell of something burning. 'This is not to be tolerated!' he would cry. 'This is *unbearable*!'

'But what's the *matter*, sir?'

'I'll tell you what's the matter,' Corkers would shout. 'Somebody's *farted*!'

'Oh no, sir!' . . . 'Not me, sir!' . . . 'Nor me, sir!' . . . 'It's none of us, sir!'

*Thanks awfully for the Tablets. I took some a few times and the indigestion has stopped now, they are jolly good*

At this point, he would rise majestically to his feet and call out at the top of his voice, '*Use door as fan! Open all windows!*'

This was the signal for frantic activity and everyone in the class would leap to his feet. It was a well-rehearsed operation and each of us knew exactly what he had to do. Four boys would man the door and begin swinging it back and forth at great speed. The rest would start clambering about on the gigantic windows which occupied one whole wall of the room, flinging the lower ones open, using a long pole with a hook on the end to open the top ones, and leaning out to gulp the fresh air in mock distress. While this was going on, Corkers would march serenely out of the room, muttering, 'It's the cabbage that does it! All they give you is disgusting cabbage and Brussels sprouts and you go off like fire-crackers!' And that was the last we saw of Corkers for the day.

But don't do that, do THIS!

# ★★★ TRICK

# The Bag of Stink

Unless you happen to have a box of **rotten eggs** or a **windy bottom** handy, smelly smells are pretty hard to come by . . . or ARE they? Here's a brilliant way to capture your own bag of stink.

**YOU WILL NEED:**
☆ One field
☆ One herd of cows
☆ One **VERY LARGE** paper bag
☆ One elastic band

What kind of animal goes 'Oom'? **A cow walking backwards.**

# WHAT YOU DO:

**1** **Stand in the next field to the cows.** (NEVER stand in the same field as a cow. Look what happened to James Henry Trotter's parents. Squashed flat by an enormous angry rhinoceros, that's what.)

**2** Hold the paper bag open and wait for the cows to – ahem – **parp**.

**3** **Catch the cow parp** (which is actually a gas called methane) in your bag then shut it tight very quickly. Secure with an elastic band.

**4** **Now choose a very important occasion** – if there is a king or queen or prime minister or president or CEO or renowned physicist or astronaut nearby that would be perfect – and then

# OPEN YOUR BAG OF STINK.

**5** **Run**. You don't want to smell the nastiness too, do you . . .?

# Spot the Mischief-maker

**Who is THIS loathsome Roald Dahl character?**

What flavour squash do Vermicious Knids like to drink? **Lemon and slime.**

**1** She has horrible laughter. **Hahahahaaaaaaargh**.

**2** She had quite a nice face when she was young . . .

**3** . . . but now she is fearfully **ugly**.

**4** She carries a **walking stick**, not to help her to walk but so that she can hit things with it, like **dogs** and **cats** and small **children**.

**5** She has a glass eye.

# Who is she?

The answer is on page 164.

How does an ogre count to 22? **On his fingers.**

# What's in Mr Twit's Beard?

**Roald Dahl didn't have a beard.** There is a very good reason for this. He **HATED** them. So when he invented the truly nasty Mr Twit, Roald Dahl gave him a **REALLY BIG** beard speckled with tiny bits of food that had once dropped out of his mouth and become stuck in the horrid hairiness.

But can you remember what WAS stuck in Mr Twit's beard? **Five of the revolting items on this page were in Mr Twit's beard.** Five weren't. But which is which?

Dried-up scrambled egg

The slimy tail of a tinned sardine

A smelly old shrimp

Mango chutney

Dollops of chocolate mousse

Mouldy old cornflake

Fried onions

Minced chicken livers

Maggoty green cheese

Last month's chicken nuggets

The answers are on page 165.

Mischievous

From Danny the Champion of the World

# Into the Wood

*In which Danny and his father risk life, limb and bottom to poach pheasants from right under the nose of the gamekeeper.*

We crouched close to the ground, watching the keeper. He was a smallish man with a cap on his head and a big double-barrelled shotgun under his arm. He never moved. He was like a little post standing there.

'Should we go?' I whispered.

The keeper's face was shadowed by the peak of his cap, but it seemed to me he was looking straight at us.

'Should we go, Dad?'

'Hush,' my father said.

Slowly, never taking his eyes from the keeper, he reached into his pocket and brought out a single raisin. He placed it in the palm of his right hand, and then quickly with a little flick of the wrist he threw the raisin high into the air. I watched it as it went sailing over the bushes and I saw it land within a yard of two hen birds standing beside an old tree-stump. Both birds turned their heads sharply at the drop of the raisin. Then one of them hopped over and made a quick peck at the ground and that must have been it.

I looked at the keeper. He hadn't moved.

I could feel a trickle of cold sweat running down one side of my forehead and across my cheek. I didn't dare lift a hand to wipe it away.

My father threw a second raisin into the clearing . . . then a third . . . and a fourth . . . and a fifth.

It takes guts to do that, I thought. Terrific guts. If I'd been alone I would never have stayed there for one second. But my father was in a sort of poacher's trance. For him, this was it. This was the moment of danger, the biggest thrill of all.

He kept on throwing the raisins into the clearing, swiftly, silently, one at a time. Flick went his wrist, and up went the raisin, high over the bushes, to land among the pheasants.

Then all at once, I saw the keeper turn away his head to inspect the wood behind him.

My father saw it too. Quick as a flash, he pulled the bag of raisins out of his pocket and tipped the whole lot into the palm of his right hand.

'Dad!' I whispered. 'Don't!'

But with a great sweep of the arm he flung the entire handful way over the bushes into the clearing.

They fell with a soft little patter, like raindrops on dry leaves, and every single pheasant in the place must have heard them fall. There was a flurry of wings and a rush to find the treasure.

The keeper's head flicked round as though there were a spring inside his neck. The birds were all pecking away madly at the raisins. The keeper took two quick paces forward, and for a moment I thought he was going in to investigate. But then he stopped, and his face came up and his eyes began travelling slowly round the edge of the clearing.

'Lie down flat!' my father whispered. 'Stay there! Don't move an inch!'

I flattened my body against the ground and pressed one side of my face into the brown leaves. The soil below the leaves had a queer pungent smell, like beer. Out of one eye, I saw my father raise his head just a tiny bit to watch the keeper. He kept watching him.

'Don't you *love* this?' he whispered to me.

I didn't dare answer him.

We lay there for what seemed like a hundred years.

At last I heard my father whisper, 'Panic's over. Follow me, Danny. But be extra careful, he's still there. And *keep down low all the time.*'

He started crawling away quickly on his hands and knees. I went after him. I kept thinking of the keeper who was somewhere behind us. I was very conscious of that keeper, and I was also very conscious of my own backside, and how it was sticking up in the air for all to see. I could understand now why 'poacher's bottom' was a fairly common complaint in this business.

We went along on our hands and knees for about a hundred yards.

'Now run!' my father said.

We got to our feet and ran, and a few minutes later we came out through the hedge into the lovely open safety of the cart-track.

'It went marvellously!' my father said, breathing heavily. 'Didn't it go absolutely marvellously?' His face was scarlet and glowing with triumph.

'Did the keeper see us?' I asked.

'Not on your life!' he said. 'And in a few minutes the sun will be going down and the birds will all be flying up to roost and that keeper will be sloping off home to his supper. Then all we've got to do is go back in again and help ourselves. We'll be picking them up off the ground like pebbles!'

He sat down on the grassy bank below the hedge. I sat down close to him. He put an arm round my shoulders and gave me a hug. 'You did well, Danny,' he said. 'I'm right proud of you.'

But don't do that, do THIS!

# ☆ TRICK

## Poach an Egg, Not a Pheasant

**Poach an egg.** (Ask an adult to help with the hot-water bit.) It's easier than poaching pheasants – and a lot more legal. Better still, boil an egg for a **REALLY good yolk**. (Ha ha! Ahem. Sorry – joke, not yolk.) Pop the hard-boiled egg back in the egg box when you're done. Then be ready to laugh **REALLY LOUDLY** when someone tries to crack it.

# Good-bye, Violet

*In which Violet Beauregarde learns that getting her own way is not ALWAYS a good idea.*

'This gum,' Mr Wonka went on, 'is my latest, my greatest, my most fascinating invention! It's a chewing-gum meal! It's ... it's ... it's ... That tiny little strip of gum lying there is a whole three-course dinner all by itself!'

'What sort of nonsense is this?' said one of the fathers.

'My dear sir!' cried Mr Wonka, 'when I start selling this gum in the shops it will change *everything*! It will be the end of all kitchens and all cooking! There will be no more shopping to do! No more buying of meat and groceries! There'll be no knives and forks at mealtimes! No plates! No washing up! No rubbish! No mess! Just a little strip of Wonka's magic chewing-gum – and that's all you'll ever need at breakfast, lunch, and supper! This piece of gum I've just made happens to be tomato soup, roast beef, and blueberry pie, but you can have almost anything you want!'

'What *do* you mean, it's tomato soup, roast beef, and blueberry pie?' said Violet Beauregarde.

'If you were to start chewing it,' said Mr Wonka, 'then that is exactly what you would get on the menu. It's absolutely amazing! You can actually *feel* the food going down your throat and into your tummy! And you can taste it perfectly! And it fills you up! It satisfies you! It's terrific!'

'It's utterly impossible,' said Veruca Salt.

'Just so long as it's gum,' shouted Violet Beauregarde, 'just so long as it's a piece of gum and I can chew it, then *that's* for me!' And quickly she took her own world-record piece of chewing-gum out of her mouth and stuck it behind her left ear. 'Come on, Mr Wonka,' she said, 'hand over this magic gum of yours and we'll see if the thing works.'

'Now, Violet,' said Mrs Beauregarde, her mother; 'don't let's do anything silly, Violet.'

'I want the gum!' Violet said obstinately. 'What's so silly?'

'I would rather you didn't take it,' Mr Wonka told her gently. 'You see, I haven't got it *quite right* yet. There are still one or two things . . .'

'Oh, to blazes with that!' said Violet, and suddenly, before Mr Wonka could stop her, she shot out a fat hand and grabbed the stick of gum out of the little drawer and popped it into her mouth. At once, her huge, well-trained jaws started chewing away on it like a pair of tongs.

'Don't!' said Mr Wonka.

'Fabulous!' shouted Violet. 'It's tomato soup! It's hot and creamy and delicious! I can feel it running down my throat!'

'Stop!' said Mr Wonka. 'The gum isn't ready yet! It's not right!'

'Of course it's right!' said Violet. 'It's working beautifully! Oh my, what lovely soup this is!'

'Spit it out!' said Mr Wonka.

'It's changing!' shouted Violet, chewing and grinning both at the same time. 'The second course is coming up! It's roast beef! It's tender and juicy! Oh boy, what a flavour! The baked potato is marvellous, too! It's got a crispy skin and it's all filled with butter inside!'

'But how *in*-teresting, Violet,' said Mrs Beauregarde. 'You are a clever girl.'

'Keep chewing, baby!' said Mr Beauregarde. 'Keep right on chewing! This is a great day for the Beauregardes! Our little girl is the first person in the world to have a chewing-gum meal!'

Everybody was watching Violet Beauregarde as she stood there chewing this extraordinary gum. Little Charlie Bucket was staring at her absolutely spellbound, watching her huge rubbery lips as they pressed and unpressed with the chewing, and

Grandpa Joe stood beside him, gaping at the girl. Mr Wonka was wringing his hands and saying, 'No, no, no, no, no! It isn't ready for eating! It isn't right! You mustn't do it!'

'Blueberry pie and cream!' shouted Violet. 'Here it comes! Oh my, it's perfect! It's beautiful! It's . . . it's exactly as though I'm swallowing it! It's as though I'm chewing and swallowing great big spoonfuls of the most marvellous blueberry pie in the world!'

'Good heavens, girl!' shrieked Mrs Beauregarde suddenly, staring at Violet, 'what's happening to your nose!'

'Oh, be quiet, mother, and let me finish!' said Violet.

'It's turning blue!' screamed Mrs Beauregarde. 'Your nose is turning blue as a blueberry!'

'Your mother is right!' shouted Mr Beauregarde. 'Your whole nose has gone purple!'

'What *do* you mean?' said Violet, still chewing away.

'Your cheeks!' screamed Mrs Beauregarde. 'They're turning blue as well! So is your chin! Your whole face is turning blue!'

'Spit that gum out at once!' ordered Mr Beauregarde.

'Mercy! Save us!' yelled Mrs Beauregarde. 'The girl's going blue and purple all over! Even her hair is changing colour! Violet, you're turning violet, Violet! What *is* happening to you?'

'I *told* you I hadn't got it quite right,' sighed Mr Wonka, shaking his head sadly.

'I'll say you haven't!' cried Mrs Beauregarde. 'Just look at the girl now!'

Everybody was staring at Violet. And what a terrible, peculiar sight she was! Her face and hands and legs and neck, in fact the skin all over her body, as well as her great big mop of curly hair, had turned a brilliant, purplish-blue, the colour of blueberry juice!

'It always goes wrong when we come to the dessert,' sighed Mr Wonka. 'It's the blueberry pie that does it. But I'll get it right one day, you wait and see.'

'Violet,' screamed Mrs Beauregarde, 'you're swelling up!'

'I feel sick,' Violet said.

'You're swelling up!' screamed Mrs Beauregarde again.

'I feel most peculiar!' gasped Violet.

'I'm not surprised!' said Mr Beauregarde.

'Great heavens, girl!' screeched Mrs Beauregarde. 'You're blowing up like a balloon!'

'Like a blueberry,' said Mr Wonka.

'Call a doctor!' shouted Mr Beauregarde.

'Prick her with a pin!' said one of the other fathers.

'Save her!' cried Mrs Beauregarde, wringing her hands.

But there was no saving her now. Her body was swelling up and changing shape at such a rate that within a minute it had turned into nothing less than

an enormous round blue ball – a gigantic blueberry, in fact – and all that remained of Violet Beauregarde herself was a tiny pair of legs and a tiny pair of arms sticking out of the great round fruit and a little head on top.

'It *always* happens like that,' sighed Mr Wonka. 'I've tried it twenty times in the Testing Room on twenty Oompa-Loompas, and every one of them finished up as a blueberry. It's most annoying. I just can't understand it.'

'But I don't want a blueberry for a daughter!' yelled Mrs Beauregarde. 'Put her back to what she was this instant!'

Mr Wonka clicked his fingers, and ten Oompa-

Loompas appeared immediately at his side.

'Roll Miss Beauregarde into the boat,' he said to them, 'and take her along to the Juicing Room at once.'

'The *Juicing Room*?' cried Mrs Beauregarde. 'What are they going to do to her there?'

'Squeeze her,' said Mr Wonka. 'We've got to squeeze the juice out of her immediately. After that, we'll just have to see how she comes out. But don't worry, my dear Mrs Beauregarde. We'll get her repaired if it's the last thing we do. I am sorry about it all, I really am . . .'

But don't do that, do THIS!

# ★★ TRICK

## Turn Yourself into a Giant Blueberry

But don't chomp on one of Willy Wonka's gourmet chewing-gum meals to turn blue, like Violet Beauregarde did. There are FAR simpler ways to make yourself look like a giant blueberry.

How do you make anti-freeze? **Steal her blanket.**

### YOU WILL NEED:

☆ A blue hat
☆ A pair of blue trousers
☆ A pair of blue socks
☆ A blue T-shirt
☆ A blue jumper
☆ 27 more blue jumpers, each one bigger than the last
☆ Blue face paint

Why shouldn't you have George's grandma for dinner? **She'd be ever so chewy.**

## WHAT YOU DO:

 Put on the blue hat, the blue trousers, the blue socks, the blue T-shirt and the 28 blue jumpers.

 Daub on the blue face paint.

 Look in a mirror.

 Ta-daaaaaaa! You're a GIANT BLUEBERRY!

**5** Now tell grown-ups that you ate too many blueberries. They will be TOTALLY fooled and think that's why you're so big and round and blue.

PS Don't try this in summer. There's nothing worse than a sweaty blueberry.

From The Witches

# The Recipe

*In which The Grand High Witch describes the spell that
will turn children into mice at PRECISELY nine o'clock
the next morning, just in time for school.*

'Attention again!' The Grand High Witch was shouting.
'I vill now give to you the rrecipe for concocting
Formula 86 Delayed Action Mouse-Maker! Get out
pencils and paper.'

Handbags were opened all over the room and
notebooks were fished out.

'Give us the recipe, O Brainy One!' cried the audience impatiently. 'Tell us the secret.'

'First,' said The Grand High Witch, 'I had to find something that vould cause the children to become very small very qvickly.'

'And what was that?' cried the audience.

'That part vos simple,' said The Grand High Witch. 'All you have to do if you are vishing to make a child very small is to look at him through the wrrrong end of a telescope.'

'She's a wonder!' cried the audience. 'Who else would have thought of a thing like that?'

'So you take the wrrrong end of a telescope,' continued The Grand High Witch, 'and you boil it until it gets soft.'

'How long does that take?' they asked her.

'Tventy-vun hours of boiling,' answered The Grand High Witch. 'And vhile this is going on, you take exactly forty-five brrrown mice and you chop off their tails vith a carving-knife and you fry the tails in hair-oil until they are nice and crrrisp.'

'What do we do with all those mice who have had their tails chopped off?' asked the audience.

'You simmer them in frog-juice for vun hour,' came the answer. 'But listen to me. So far I have only given you the easy part of the rrrecipe. The rrreally difficult problem is to put in something that vill have a genuine delayed action rrree-sult, something that  can be eaten by children on a certain day but vhich vill not start vurrrking on them until nine o'clock the next morning vhen they arrive at school.'

'What did you come up with, O Brainy One?' they called out. 'Tell us the great secret!'

'The secret,' announced The Grand High Witch triumphantly, 'is an *alarm-clock*!'

'An alarm-clock!' they cried. 'It's a stroke of genius!'

'Of course it is,' said The Grand High Witch.

'You can set a tventy-four-hour alarm-clock today and at exactly nine o'clock tomorrow it vill go off.'

'But we will need five million alarm-clocks!' cried the audience. 'We will need one for each child!'

'Idiots!' shouted The Grand High Witch. 'If you are vonting a steak, you do not cook the whole cow! It is the same vith alarm-clocks. Vun clock vill make enough for a thousand children. Here is vhat you do. You set your alarm-clock to go off at nine o'clock tomorrow morning.

Then you rrroast it in the oven until it is crrrisp and
tender. Are you wrrriting this down?'

'We are, Your Grandness, we are!' they cried.

'Next,' said The Grand High Witch, 'you take your
boiled telescope and your frrried mouse-tails and your
cooked mice and your rrroasted alarm-clock and all
together you put them into the mixer. Then you mix

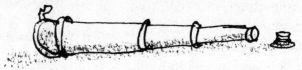

them at full speed. This vill give you a nice thick paste.
Vhile the mixer is still mixing you must add to it the
yolk of vun grrruntle's egg.'

'A gruntle's egg!' cried the audience. 'We shall do
that!'

 Underneath all the clamour that was
going on I heard one witch in the back
row saying to her neighbour, 'I'm
getting a bit old to go bird's nesting.
Those ruddy gruntles always nest very high up.'

'So you mix in the egg,' The
Grand High Witch went
on, 'and vun after the
other you also mix in the
following items: the claw

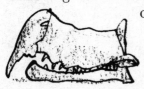

of a crrrabcrrruncher, the beak
of a blabbersnitch, the snout
of a grrrobblesqvirt and the
tongue of a catsprrringer.

I trust you are not having any trrrouble finding those.'

'None at all!' they cried out. 'We will spear the blabbersnitch and trap the crabcruncher and shoot the grobblesquirt and catch the catspringer in his burrow!'

'Excellent!' said The Grand High Witch. 'Vhen you have mixed everything together in the mixer, you vill have a most marvellous-looking grrreen liqvid. Put vun drop, just vun titchy droplet, of this liqvid into a chocolate or a sveet, and *at nine o'clock the next morning* the child who ate it vill turn into a mouse in twenty-six seconds! But vun vurd of vorning. Never increase the dose. Never put more than vun drrrop into each sveet or chocolate. And never give more than vun sweet or chocolate to each child. An overdose of Delayed Action Mouse-Maker vill mess up the timing of the alarm-clock and cause the child to turn into a mouse too early. A large overdose might even have an instant effect, and you vouldn't vont that, vould you? You vouldn't vont the children turning into mice rrright there in your sveet-shops. That vould give the game away. So be very carrreful! Do not overdose!'

But don't do that, do THIS!

# TRICK

## The
# Great Mouse Trick

### THE GRAND HIGH WITCH'S
### Formula 86 Delayed Action Mouse-Maker

is probably not a spell you want to cast on your friends. (Not if you ever want them to speak – or even **SQUEAK** – to you again.) Instead, try this harmless yet **HILARIOUS** trick. All you need to do is stick a tiny piece of sticky tape over the optical sensor underneath a computer mouse and, as if by magic, it won't work.

PS This would usually be labelled a one-star trick. The extra star is awarded because of the high risk of sending grown-ups **STARK STARING BONKERS** when they discover that their computer doesn't work properly. If your particular adult displays danger signs – **turns beetroot**, **starts growling**, **stamps feet**, **shouts a lot** – suggest that they turn the computer off and on again while you secretly remove the sticky tape . . . and then declare yourself a **computer genius**!

# Boggis's Chicken House
## Number One

*In which Mr Fox and his four children bravely tunnel
to Chicken House Number One to find their dinner.*

'This time we must go in a very special direction,' said
Mr Fox, pointing sideways and downward.

So he and his four children started to dig once
again. The work went much more slowly now. Yet
they kept at it with great courage, and little by little
the tunnel began to
grow.

'Dad, I
wish you
would tell us
*where* we are
going,' said
one of the
children.

'I dare not do that,' said Mr Fox, 'because this place I am *hoping* to get to is so *marvellous* that if I described it to you now you would go crazy with excitement. And then, if we failed to get there (which is very possible), you would die of disappointment. I don't want to raise your hopes too much, my darlings.'

For a long long time they kept on digging. For how long they did not know, because there were no days and no nights down there in the murky tunnel. But at last Mr Fox gave the order to stop. 'I think,' he said, 'we had better take a peep upstairs now and see where we are. I know where I *want* to be, but I can't possibly be sure we're anywhere near it.'

Slowly, wearily, the foxes began to slope the tunnel up towards the surface. Up and up it went . . . until suddenly they came to something hard above their heads and they couldn't go up any further. Mr Fox reached up to examine this hard thing. 'It's wood!' he whispered. 'Wooden planks!'

'What does that mean, Dad?'

'It means, unless I am very much mistaken, that we are right underneath somebody's house,' whispered Mr Fox. 'Be very quiet now while I take a peek.'

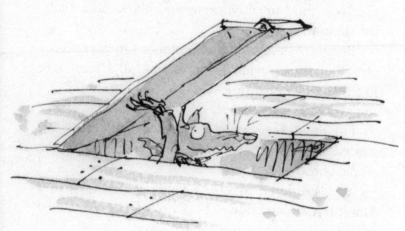

Carefully, Mr Fox began pushing up one of the floorboards. The board creaked most terribly and they all ducked down, waiting for something awful to happen. Nothing did. So Mr Fox pushed up a second board. And then, very very cautiously, he poked his head up through the gap. He let out a shriek of excitement.

'*I've done it!*' he yelled. 'I've done it *first time*! *I've done it! I've done it!*' He pulled himself up through the gap in the floor and started prancing and dancing with joy. 'Come on up!' he sang out. 'Come up and see where you are, my darlings! What a sight for a hungry fox! Hallelujah! Hooray! Hooray!'

The four Small Foxes scrambled up out of the tunnel and what a fantastic sight it was that now met their eyes! They were in a huge shed and the whole place was teeming with chickens. There were white chickens and brown chickens and black chickens by the thousand!

'Boggis's Chicken House Number One!' cried Mr Fox. 'It's exactly what I was aiming at! I hit it slap in the middle! First time! Isn't that fantastic! *And*, if I may say so, rather clever!'

The Small Foxes went wild with excitement. They started running around in all directions, chasing the stupid chickens.

'Wait!' ordered Mr Fox. 'Don't lose your heads! Stand back! Calm down! Let's do this properly! First of all, everyone have a drink of water!'

They all ran over to the chickens' drinking-trough and lapped up the lovely cool water. Then Mr Fox chose three of the plumpest hens, and with a clever flick of his jaws he killed them instantly.

'Back to the tunnel!' he ordered. 'Come on! No fooling around! The quicker you move, the quicker you shall have something to eat!'

One after another, they climbed down through

the hole in the floor and soon they were all standing
once again in the dark tunnel. Mr Fox reached up
and pulled the floorboards back into place. He
did this with great care. He did it so that no
one could tell they had ever been
moved.

**But don't do
that, do THIS!**

# ★★★ TRICK

## How to Steal a Prehistoric Creature

If you're reading this book, there's a big chance you're not a fox. So there's really no need for you to steal a chicken. (Besides, you can buy them in all good supermarkets.) Instead, why not go for something **HYSTERICALLY historical**, like . . . a **DODO**!

> **YOU WILL NEED:**
> ☆ One time machine
> ☆ One sherry trifle
> ☆ One net

What do you call a swarm of monster bees? **Zombees.**

## WHAT YOU DO:

**1** **Construct a time machine.**
(At the time of writing, there were no instructions available for how to make a time machine, but we are reasonably confident that you could knock one up using a **large glass box** – rather like the one from *Charlie and the Great Glass Elevator* – **a large ball of string, a gearstick from a 1979 Mini 1275GT, a Mars bar, a crystal ball and a jetpack**.)

**2** **Make a sherry trifle.**

**3** **Set the time machine to any date before 1662,** which is when the dodo was last spotted before becoming extinct FOREVER.

**4** **Travel through time.**

**5** **Land.**

**6** Disembark the time machine and **locate your dodo**. (Don't worry about it flying away. It can't.)

**7** Lure the dodo into your time machine with the **sherry trifle**. (No records exist confirming that dodos liked sherry trifle, but WHO DOESN'T?)

**8** Travel back through time to **NOW**.

**9** **Take the dodo to a top zoologist** and become famous for bringing the world's most fabulous flightless bird back from the dead.

**10** There – that's more exciting than stealing a chicken, isn't it?

# Spot the Mischief-maker

**Who is this mischievous chap from one of Roald Dahl's marvellous storybooks?**

What's a rabbit's favourite music?
**Hip hop.**

**1** His father is a **farmer**.

**2** He likes **chocolate**.

**3** He doesn't like **cabbage**.

**4** He's a **brave** little boy.

**5** He doesn't have a **brother** or a **sister**.

# Who is he?

The answer is on page 164.

# True or False

Which of these **tricks** did Roald Dahl actually do in **true life** and which are **TOTAL FIBS**?

**1** He climbed a ladder up to his daughters' bedroom, poked a bamboo cane between the curtains and pretended to be the **BFG**.

**2** He invented an everlasting gobstopper and tricked the great Quentin Blake into sucking it for **THREE WEEKS**.

**3** He hid A DEAD MOUSE in a jar of sweets in a sweetshop.

**4** He once pretended to be the president of the USA and governed the country for one morning in November 1969.

**5** He rigged up a zipwire and used it to **waterbomb** two unsuspecting ladies.

The answers are on page 166.

# Little Red Riding Hood and the Wolf

*In which Roald Dahl twists and turns and warps and bends the well-known story of Little Red Riding Hood into something QUITE different.*

As soon as Wolf began to feel
That he would like a decent meal,
He went and knocked on Grandma's door.
When Grandma opened it, she saw
The sharp white teeth, the horrid grin,
And Wolfie said, 'May I come in?'
Poor Grandmamma was terrified,
'He's going to eat me up,' she cried.
And she was absolutely right.
He ate her up in one big bite.
But Grandmamma was small and tough,
And Wolfie wailed, 'That's not enough!
'I haven't yet begun to feel

'That I have had a decent meal!'
He ran around the kitchen yelping,
'I've *got* to have another helping!'

Then added with a frightful leer,
'I'm therefore going to wait right here
'Till Little Miss Red Riding Hood
'Comes home from walking in the wood.'
He quickly put on Grandma's clothes.
(Of course he hadn't eaten those.)
He dressed himself in coat and hat.

He put on shoes and after that
He even brushed and curled his hair,
Then sat himself in Grandma's chair.
In came the little girl in red.
She stopped. She stared. And then she said,

*'What great big ears you have, Grandma.'*
*'All the better to hear you with,'* the Wolf replied.

'*What great big eyes you have, Grandma,*'
    said Little Red Riding Hood.
'*All the better to see you with,*' the Wolf replied.

He sat there watching her and smiled.
He thought, I'm going to eat this child.
Compared with her old Grandmamma
She's going to taste like caviare.

Then Little Red Riding Hood said, '*But Grandma,*
*what a lovely great big furry coat you have on.*'

'That's wrong!' cried Wolf. 'Have you forgot
'To tell me what BIG TEETH I've got?
'Ah well, no matter what you say,
'I'm going to eat you anyway.'
The small girl smiles. One eyelid flickers.
She whips a pistol from her knickers.
She aims it at the creature's head
And *bang bang bang*, she shoots him dead.
A few weeks later, in the wood,
I came across Miss Riding Hood.
But what a change! No cloak of red,
No silly hood upon her head.
She said, 'Hello, and do please note
'My lovely furry WOLFSKIN COAT.'

But don't do that, do THIS!

# ⭐ TRICK

## Red Riding Hoody

### 𝕽𝖊𝖉 𝖗𝖎𝖉𝖎𝖓𝖌 𝖍𝖔𝖔𝖉𝖘

are SO century-before-last. Update your look and **swap that red cape for a red hoody**. Get one for your grandmamma while you're at it. Then you can both easily trick the Wolf into thinking you're not

*Little Red Riding Hood*

and Grandmamma at all and would be nowhere near as **delicious** as either of them. AND you'll be warm. (And VERY cool at the same time.) But if you really want to avoid being eaten, it's probably best not to live in a wooden cottage in the deep, dark woods at all. **It's the first place a wolf looks for his lunch.**

From The Twits

# The Glass Eye

*In which Mrs Twit shows Mr Twit that she has eyes EVERYWHERE.*

You can play a lot of tricks with a glass eye because you can take it out and pop it back in again any time you like. You can bet your life Mrs Twit knew all the tricks.

One morning she took out her glass eye and dropped it into Mr Twit's mug of beer when he wasn't looking.

Mr Twit sat there drinking the beer slowly. The froth made a white ring on the hairs around his mouth. He wiped the white froth on to his sleeve and wiped his sleeve on his trousers.

'You're plotting something,' Mrs Twit said, keeping her back turned so he wouldn't see that she had taken out her glass eye. 'Whenever you go all quiet like that I know very well you're plotting something.'

Mrs Twit was right. Mr Twit was plotting away like mad. He was trying to think up a really nasty trick he could play on his wife that day.

'You'd better be careful,' Mrs Twit said, 'because when I see you starting to plot, I watch you like a wombat.'

'Oh, do shut up, you old hag,' Mr Twit said. He went on drinking his beer, and his evil mind kept working away on the latest horrid trick he was going to play on the old woman.

Suddenly, as Mr Twit tipped the last drop of beer down his throat, he caught sight of Mrs Twit's awful glass eye staring up at him from the bottom of the mug. It made him jump.

'I told you I was watching you,' cackled Mrs Twit. 'I've got eyes everywhere so you'd better be careful.'

But don't do that, do THIS!

# ☆ TRICK

## The Joke Eye

 You don't need a glass eye to play the same trick as Mrs Twit. Oh no. Here's a much tastier alternative.

**YOU WILL NEED:**
- ☆ One lychee (a fancy white fruit that looks VERY like an eyeball and tastes DELICIOUS)
- ☆ One green olive
- ☆ One raisin
- ☆ One teaspoon
- ☆ One cocktail stick or toothpick

What do you call an alien with three eyes?
**An aliiien.**

## WHAT YOU DO:

**1** Using your teaspoon, **hollow out the lychee** until you have made an **olive-sized hole**.

**2** Put the olive into the hole.

**3** Now use your cocktail stick or toothpick to make a **raisin-sized hole in the olive**.

**4** Put the raisin into the hole.

**5** *Voilà*! You've made a **joke eye**! The lychee is the white of the eye, the olive the iris and the raisin the pupil.

**6** Now all you have to do is pop the joke eye in your unsuspecting victim's drink and wait for them to
# SCREEEEEEEEEEEEAM!

# The Frog

*In which Mr Twit pays back Mrs Twit for putting a glass eye in his beer by hiding a Giant Skillywiggler in her bed.*

To pay her back for the glass eye in his beer, Mr Twit decided he would put a frog in Mrs Twit's bed.

He caught a big one down by the pond and carried it back secretly in a box.

That night, when Mrs Twit was in the bathroom getting ready for bed, Mr Twit slipped the frog between her sheets. Then he got into his own bed and waited for the fun to begin.

Mrs Twit came back and climbed into her bed and put out the light. She lay there in the dark scratching her tummy. Her tummy was itching. Dirty old hags like her always have itchy tummies.

Then all at once she felt something cold and slimy crawling over her feet. She screamed.

'What's the matter with you?' Mr Twit said.

'Help!' screamed Mrs Twit, bouncing about. 'There's something in my bed!'

'I'll bet it's that Giant Skillywiggler I saw on the floor just now,' Mr Twit said.

'That *what*?' screamed Mrs Twit.

'I tried to kill it but it got away,' Mr Twit said. 'It's got teeth like screwdrivers!'

'Help!' screamed Mrs Twit. 'Save me! It's all over my feet!'

'It'll bite off your toes,' said Mr Twit.

Mrs Twit fainted.

Mr Twit got out of bed and fetched a jug of cold water. He poured the water over Mrs Twit's head to revive her. The frog crawled up from under the sheets to get near the water. It started jumping about on the pillow. Frogs love water. This one was having a good time.

When Mrs Twit came to, the frog had just jumped on to her face. This is not a nice thing to happen to anyone in bed at night. She screamed again.

'By golly it *is* a Giant Skillywiggler!' Mr Twit said. 'It'll bite off your nose.'

Mrs Twit leapt out of bed and flew downstairs and spent the night on the sofa. The frog went to sleep on her pillow.

But don't do that, do THIS!

# ★★ TRICK

## Hedgehog Bed

**Giant Skillywigglers** (and frogs) are a little hard to come by and they can **REALLY** muck up a matching duvet-and-pillowcase set. For fabulously **NON-GLOOPY** fun, simply pop a selection of brushes under someone's pillow or inside their duvet cover. Any sort of brush will do – **hairbrushes, toothbrushes, nailbrushes, scrubbing brushes, paintbrushes, dustpan brushes** . . .

**Before bedtime**, mention that you've heard mad hedgehogs are on the loose in the area. Then when your victim discovers the prickles in the middle of the night, they'll think a mad hedgehog is **IN THEIR BED**.

# Something Nasty in the Lifts

*In which Charlie Bucket and Mr and Mrs Bucket and
Grandpa Jo and Grandma Josephine and Grandpa George and
Grandma Georgina and Willy Wonka meet ONE OF THE
SCARIEST ALIENS IN THE UNIVERSE. Yikes!*

It looked more than anything like an enormous egg
balanced on its pointed end. It was as tall as a big boy
and wider than the fattest man. The greenish-brown
skin had a shiny wettish appearance and there were
wrinkles in it. About three-quarters of the way up, in
the widest part, there were two large round eyes as
big as tea-cups. The eyes were white, but each had a
brilliant red pupil in the centre. The red pupils were
resting on Mr Wonka. But now they began travelling
slowly across to Charlie and Grandpa Joe and the
others by the bed, settling upon them and gazing at
them with a cold malevolent stare. The eyes were
everything. There were no other features, no nose or

mouth or ears, but the entire egg-shaped body was itself moving very very slightly, pulsing and bulging gently here and there as though the skin were filled with some thick fluid.

At this point, Charlie suddenly noticed that the next lift was coming down. The indicator numbers above the door were flashing . . . 6 . . . 5 . . . 4 . . . 3 . . . 2 . . . 1 . . . L (for lobby). There was a slight pause. The door slid open and there, inside the second lift, was another enormous slimy wrinkled greenish-brown egg with eyes!

Now the numbers were flashing above all three of the remaining lifts. Down they came . . . down . . . down . . . down . . . And soon, at precisely the same time, they reached the lobby floor and the doors slid open . . . five open doors now . . . one creature in each . . . five in all . . . and five pairs of eyes with brilliant red centres all watching Mr Wonka and watching Charlie and Grandpa Joe and the others.

There were slight differences in size and shape between the five, but all had the same greenish-brown wrinkled skin and the skin was rippling and pulsing.

For about thirty seconds nothing happened. Nobody stirred, nobody made a sound. The silence was terrible. So was the suspense. Charlie was so frightened he felt himself shrinking inside his skin. Then he saw the creature in the left-hand lift suddenly starting to change shape! Its body was slowly becoming longer and longer, and thinner and thinner, going up and up towards the roof of the lift, not straight up, but curving a little to the left, making a snake-like curve that was curiously graceful, up to the left and then curling over the top to the right and coming down again in a half-circle . . . and then the bottom end began to grow out as well, like a tail . . . creeping along the floor . . . creeping along the floor to the left . . . until at last the creature, which had originally looked like a huge egg, now looked like a long curvy serpent standing up on its tail.

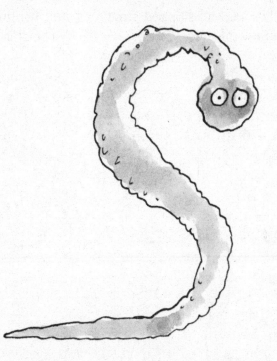

Then the one in the next lift began stretching itself in much the same way, and what a weird and oozy thing it was to watch! It was twisting itself into a shape that was a bit different from the first, balancing itself almost but not quite on the tip of its tail.

Then the three remaining creatures began stretching themselves all at the same time, each one elongating itself slowly upward, growing taller and taller, thinner and thinner, curving and twisting, stretching and stretching, curling and bending, balancing either on the tail or the head or both, and turned sideways now so that only one eye was visible.

When they had all stopped stretching and bending,
this was how they finished up:

'*Scram!*' shouted Mr Wonka. 'Get out quick!'

People have never moved faster than Grandpa Joe
and Charlie and Mr and Mrs Bucket at that moment.
They all got behind the bed and started pushing
like crazy. Mr Wonka ran in front of them shouting
'Scram! Scram! Scram!' and in ten seconds flat all of

them were out of the lobby and back inside the Great Glass Elevator. Frantically, Mr Wonka began undoing bolts and pressing buttons. The door of the Great Glass Elevator snapped shut and the whole thing leaped sideways. They were away! And of course all of them, including the three old ones in the bed, floated up again into the air.

But don't do that, do THIS!

# TRiCK

## The Daring Plan to Trap a Vermicious Knid

By now, you must be fairly accomplished at carrying out **plots**, **plans**, **japes** and **jokes**, but this is a plan to test even the most experienced mischief-maker. You're going to trap a **Vermicious Knid**. Fail and you'll be, um . . . Well, let's not go into that here. Succeed and you'll be made a knight or a dame or, at the very least, a very important person with a certificate to prove it **RIGHT AWAY**. (Probably.)

### YOU WILL NEED:

☆ One spacesuit and helmet (help the environment by re-using the spacesuit and helmet from **The Sticky Rocket** on page 40)
☆ One space rocket
☆ One oval gilt-edged mirror and superglue
☆ One butterfly net
☆ One good book (*Charlie and the Great Glass Elevator* is perfect)
☆ One MP3 player (with speakers) loaded with some beautiful love songs

# WHAT YOU DO:

1. Wearing the **spacesuit and helmet**, climb on-board the rocket and blast off in the direction of **deep space**.

2. Settle down with your good book. (Luckily, the time it will take you to read *Charlie and the Great Glass Elevator* is EXACTLY the length of time it takes to reach deep space, at a velocity of a **zillion kilometres per hour**.)

3. When you have reached **deep space**, select and play the love songs.

4. Glue the mirror to the rocket's outer wall.

5. **Wait.**

6. **You might have to wait quite a while.**

7. When the **Vermicious Knid** sees itself in the mirror, it will be stunned by its own beauty and **FREEZE**!

8. Quickly whip out the net from its hiding place and plonk it right over the **Vermicious Knid**.

9. Fly back to **planet Earth**.

10. Take the butterfly net to **London**, **England**.

11. Go to Buckingham Palace. Ask to see the **Queen**.

12. The Queen, who knows a lot about strange beings after her dealings with the **BFG**, will immediately invite you to afternoon tea. The Vermicious Knid, on the other hand, will be sent straight to London Zoo. **Job done.**

# Spot the Mischief-maker

**Can you identify this HUMONGOUS character?**

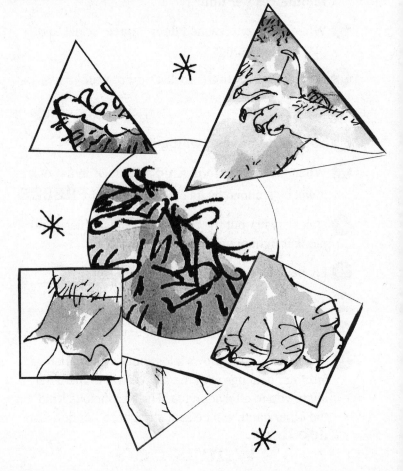

**1**

He is **naked** apart from a sort of short skirt around his waist. (Oh, I say.)

**2**

He is simply **colossal**, with a **large belly**, **long arms** and **VERY big feet** (so ginormous that you absolutely wouldn't be able to find shoes to fit on the high street).

**3**

He has tiny **piggy black eyes**.

What goes ha-ha-ha-ha-ha thud? **A monster laughing its head off.**

**4**

**He eats human beans.**

**5**

The only person in the whole wide world who can outwit him is a sweet girl called **Sophie**.

# Who is he?

The answer is on page 164.

# Vile Endings

Can you match up the **vile character** with the way that Roald Dahl **dispatched** them?

 He was **sizzled** up like a sausage.

 They were ironed out upon the grass as **flat** and **thin** and lifeless as a couple of **paper dolls** cut out of a picture book.

 They were sentenced to a lifetime of **snozzcumbers**.

They got the **DREADED** SHRINKS.

She did a **bunk**.

The answers are on page 166.

# Afterword

# What?

It's the end of the book **ALREADY**? **Wow**. Doesn't time fly when you're gluing a rocket to a launchpad! Did you enjoy reading about the **mischief** and **mayhem** that Roald Dahl created in his fiction and in real life too? We do hope so, because this is the sort of **extreme trickery** that Roald Dahl was all about. He loved it when he was a schoolboy; he loved it when he was very grown-up indeed. Perhaps you love it too. Perhaps that's why you've read this book. And PERHAPS you're going to go away and create your very own **mischief**, right now. And **mayhem**, of course.

**Don't forget the mayhem.**

# Answers

## SPOT THE MISCHIEF-MAKER

**Pages 42–43:** It's WILLY WONKA from *Charlie and the Chocolate Factory* and *Charlie and the Great Glass Elevator*, of course!

**Pages 66–67:** Mr Fox from *Fantastic Mr Fox*.

**Pages 100–101:** Mrs Twit! Did you get it or are YOU a twit too?

**Pages 132–133:** George Kranky from *George's Marvellous Medicine*.

**Pages 160–161:** It is, of course, Fleshlumpeater, one of the most loathsome giants from *The BFG*. (But award yourself half a point if you guessed another one of the giants. They're all fairly big and horrid and easy to mix up.)

## Page 44:
## GOOEY QUESTIONS
**❶** A Whipple-Scrumptious Fudgemallow Delight
**❷** Prince Pondicherry
**❸** Dark brown gloss paint
**❹** He glued the branches of the Big Dead Tree.

## Page 68:
## TERRIBLE TRICKS
**❶** Augustus Gloop
**❷** Veruca Salt
**❸** Mike Teavee
**❹** Violet Beauregarde

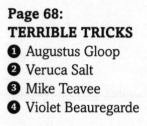

## PAGE 102:
## WHAT'S IN MR TWIT'S BEARD?
*IN THE BEARD:*
Dried-up scrambled egg
Minced chicken livers
Maggoty green cheese
Mouldy old cornflake
The slimy tail of a
tinned sardine

*NOT IN THE BEARD:*
A smelly old shrimp
Dollops of chocolate mousse
Last month's chicken nuggets
Mango chutney
Fried onions

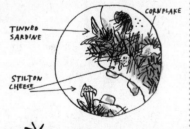

### Page 134:
### TRUE OR FALSE
❶ TRUE
❷ FALSE
❸ TRUE
❹ FALSE
❺ TRUE

### Page 162:
### VILE ENDINGS
❶ The Enormous Crocodile
❷ Aunt Sponge and Aunt Spiker
❸ The nasty giants from *The BFG*
❹ Mr and Mrs Twit
❺ Miss Trunchbull

# THERE'S MORE TO ROALD DAHL
# THAN GREAT STORIES . . .

**Did you know that 10% of author royalties\* from this book go to help the work of the Roald Dahl charities?**

**Roald Dahl's Marvellous Children's Charity** exists to make life better for seriously ill children because it believes that every child has the right to a marvellous life.

This marvellous charity helps thousands of children each year living with serious conditions of the blood and the brain – causes important to Roald Dahl in his lifetime – whether by providing nurses, equipment or toys for today's children in the UK, or helping tomorrow's children everywhere through pioneering research.

Can you do something marvellous to help others?
Find out how at **www.marvellouschildrenscharity.org**

**The Roald Dahl Museum and Story Centre**, based in Great Missenden just outside London, is in the Buckinghamshire village where Roald Dahl lived and wrote. At the heart of the Museum, created to inspire a love of reading and writing, is his unique archive of letters and manuscripts. As well as two fun-packed biographical galleries, the Museum boasts an interactive Story Centre. It is a place for the family, teachers and their pupils to explore the exciting world of creativity and literacy.
**www.roalddahlmuseum.org**

# Read more from Roald Dahl,

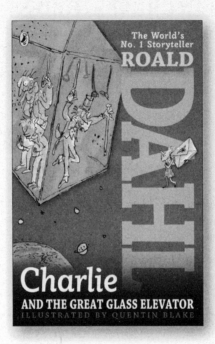

## Now that he's won the chocolate factory, what's next for Charlie?

Last seen flying through the sky in a giant elevator in *Charlie and the Chocolate Factory*, Charlie Bucket's back for another adventure. When the giant elevator picks up speed, Charlie, Willy Wonka, and the gang are sent hurtling through space and time. Visiting the world's first space hotel, battling the dreaded Vermicious Knids, and saving the world are only a few stops along this remarkable, intergalactic joyride.

# the World's No. 1 Storyteller!

## "The Trunchbull" is no match for Matilda!

Matilda is a sweet, exceptional young girl, but her parents think she's just a nuisance. She expects school to be different, but there she has to face Miss Trunchbull, a kid-hating terror of a headmistress. When Matilda is attacked by the Trunchbull, she suddenly discovers she has a remarkable power with which to fight back. It'll take a superhuman genius to give Miss Trunchbull what she deserves, and Matilda may be just the one to do it!

## Captured by a giant!

The BFG is no ordinary bone-crunching giant. He is far too nice and jumbly. It's lucky for Sophie that he is. Had she been carried off in the middle of the night by the Bloodbottler, or any of the other giants—rather than the BFG—she would have soon become breakfast. When Sophie hears that the giants are flush-bunking off to England to swollomp a few nice little chiddlers, she decides she must stop them once and for all. And the BFG is going to help her!